This book is printed using opendyslexic, an open-source font, provided by opendyslexic.org, that's made to help with readability. Please support their effort.

SOMETIMES KAT,
SOMETIMES KEV

Mx. Knowitall

DreamPunk Press
www.dreampunkpress.com

Sometimes Kat, Sometimes Kev

Cover design by Morven Moeller

2nd Edition
OpenDyslexic font

ISBN: 978-1-938215-33-9

Categories: LGBT-Fiction, SAGA-Fiction, Gay-Fiction, Transgender-Fiction, Gender-fluid-Fiction, Alien-Fiction, Sci-Fi-Fiction

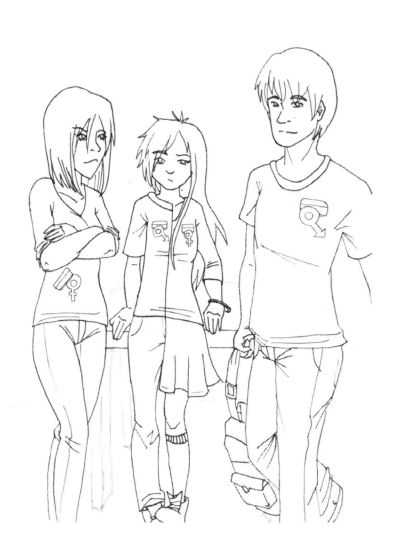

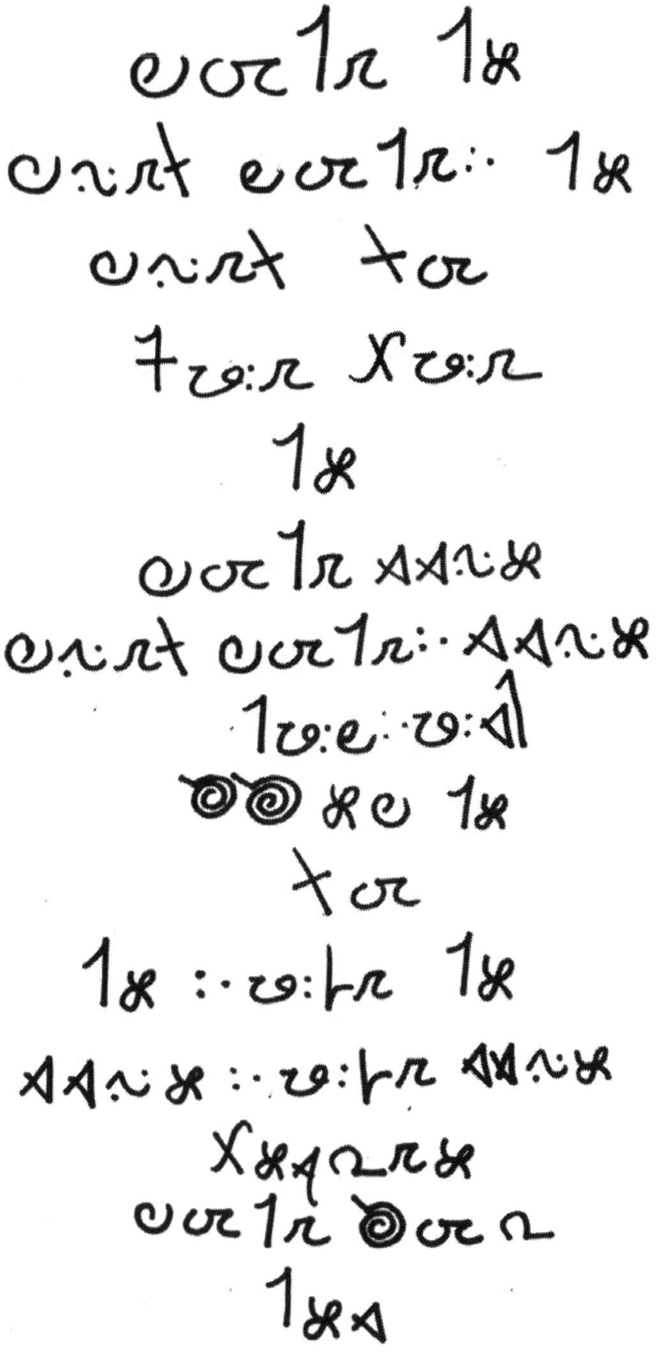

CHAPTER ONE

Living in a small town is not much fun. Everyone knows everyone and the least little things in their days. I know that Mrs. Howard, my 5th grade teacher is currently having an affair with my 10th grade math teacher, Ms. Freeman. I know that the Chief of Police is at the slots in Las Vegas for just over a week every month; and I know that the new girl at school, that hasn't even set an eye on or foot in the school, is really pretty.

Just some things that get around the town.

Just some things can't get around the town.

"Hey, Kevin, wanna come over? I figured we could make some pizza... well you could anyway, and we could laze around and hang out." Bryan, my best friend in the whole world, my only ally in my small town, is always up for lazing and pizza... at least, when I make it.

I shook my head. "Sure, let me ask my mom." I hold the phone away from my face and call out to my mother. When she doesn't answer, I return the phone to my ear. "Yeah, I can go, what time?"

I heard a crash on the other end of the line. "Whenever." I then heard another crash.

I sighed, making sure it was directly into the phone. "Sooner rather than later?" I figured he

1

would probably want help cleaning whatever he just messed up or broke.

"Preferably."

I nodded on my side of the phone. "See you soon."

"Yep." The receiver clicked and the dialtone sounded.

I smiled and rushed up stairs to grab my clothes. Why? Because, I would probably end up staying the night.

Up in my room, I giggled for no reason at all and jammed all the clothes I could carry into my gym bag. I was almost done packing when a high dinging sound reverberated through my room. I immediately jumped and rushed to my closet. You see, I had a box in there with a bunch of stuff that my parents received when they got me. A few laser pointers and a few tazer guns, but this beeping came from a doohicky in the back corner, with a hologram popped up from it. The Hologram read, 'Match Detected'.

I grabbed it and started pressing buttons frantically, trying to get it to stop beeping so loud. Because, if something was loud, people noticed. And when people noticed, people talked. In a town like mine, small, endangered, bored, talking was a dangerous thing. It stopped beeping and the hologram disappeared.

Especially to those with a secret.

I rushed out of the house and down the street. I needed to talk to Bryan about this; he would have some weird and crazed explanation that, in the long run, would help me to understand the truth.

I turned one corner and slowed up. What if he wanted to talk about his girlfriend or that guy that was trying to beat me up on Monday, though? I hope he wasn't planning on talking about those mundane things.

I should really look where I'm going, because I ran into someone. A very pretty someone. A hot someone... someone I didn't know, and in a small town, you know everyone. Everyone knows you, or, at least, they think they do.

I watched helplessly; all of the things in her hands fell harmoniously to the sidewalk, some crunching in bags and others sloshing in plastic containers. I took a moment to guess what each of them was before speaking. What looked like caramel with lumpy, maggot-like textures. What looked like 'oobleck' from the Dr. Seuss book. What seemed to be a green and blue mixture of oil and water because, after their fall, they were separating again. "I'm so sorry, I really should look where I'm going," I bent down and started picking up jars and bags.

She squatted down awkwardly in what seemed to be jeans that were way too tight and a shirt that was way too short and a thong that showed way too much. I swallowed. Boys have imaginations, and girls are a big part of those imaginations. "No, no it's fine. I really should have been holding them better or... packed them better."

I nodded, not really listening, but I would remember what she said later. "So, you're the new girl in town."

She nodded. She licked her lips and tucked her hair behind an ear.

I'm observant, I know I'm observant, but I think she was doing all of it on purpose and I didn't care.

"I was hoping to meet everyone tomorrow at school. You know, small town," she pointed at herself, "new girl," she pointed at me, "in a very *small* town."

I found myself nodding along with her delightful voice. I also felt a delightful feeling in the pit of my stomach and in the nougatty filling of my chest where she just pointed at me. "Well, I hope nothing has been too weird or out of the ordinary or troublesome since you arrived."

She cocked her head to the side. I think I mimicked her afterward. "Alright."

I just stood there. Thinking back, I was probably the most awkward thing since she moved into the house. I still don't care, though.

"Well, I should get these into the house. I told my mom I would be in for dinner." It sounded more like a question than it was probably supposed to.

I nodded one last time before she turned with her bin of out-of-the-ordinary items and walked toward the house. I didn't move though. She was walking away with way too tight jeans, a way to short shirt, and a way to much showing thong. I watched long enough to memorize it, in case I never got to see it again.

Bryan was waiting on his porch when I got there. He was rocking a wicker chair onto two legs then balancing with his feet on the pristine white railing.

I tutted at him while I skipped up the walkway; well, partially up the walkway. The walkway, actually, meanders a bit, swirling through different flowers and ornamental shrubs that serve no use but to wear down people's arches with extra walking. I took the shortcut, jumping over the shrubs that block the twists in the walk.

"Why were you so long? I'm hungry."

Leave it for Bryan to complain about my tardiness and his stomach in the same breath.

5

"I'm here now." I vaulted up the steps in a single leap and stood at the edge of the front deck glaring at him. "Where will I find the stuff to make your pizza?"

He lowered the hovering front legs of the chair so that he could stand next to me. I smiled as he stuffed his hands into his pockets. "On the island in the paper bags. But seriously, where were you; don't you usually come straight over?" He followed me into the house, down the hall to the kitchen and the island.

Bryan's house had a wonderful kitchen. Most of it was red and filled with energy. There was a stainless steel wall that reached out with fingers enveloping parts of the next wall as well. A double oven, a full freezer then full fridge, even a stove top and hood all of a foggy-mirror metal. I unpacked the paper bags and trudged over to the cabinet filled with trays and pans 'safe for conventional oven use'.

"I ran into someone." I wanted to bring up the new girl, that I had no name for or any other way to define her... other than a black thong. I reached for the pizza stone and found, the hard way, that I was too short to reach the upper shelf in the cabinet. I huffed.

"Ran into who?"

I jumped; Bryan was a lot closer than he was a moment ago. I immediately spun around and pressed

6

my back into the pantry door under the shelf, the too-high shelf. I felt like my throat had closed up. "Uh... the new girl." I swallowed hoping the lump would go away, but it was persistent.

He reached up to the pizza tray. I spent the time looking at his Adam's apple that was level with my eyes. It bobbed up and down.

It took me a moment to realize that he had spoken. "Sorry?"

He placed the pizza stone in my hands and turned to sit on one of the stools around the island. "I said, 'Really?'"

I nodded and followed him to the island. He had already cut the packaging on the raw pizza dough. I pulled out a knife and rolled the tomatoes toward me. I smiled to myself when he began to spread the dough with his fingers; he had learned to start spreading the dough. I taught him, and now he does it without me asking. "Yeah, she was carrying some odd-ball things, like, really weird stuff.

Bryan gave a breathy laugh. "Weird for you must be completely off-the-deep-end for me, yeah?" He swiveled the stone and kept spreading the dough.

I swallowed. "Well, I don't know. There was stuff like grainy pudding that wasn't any color I had seen before and some mealy-looking fruits or something that didn't seem natural. Weird, yes. Off the deep end? I wouldn't think so. You're totally cool with me so why would that be even weirder?"

Bryan laughed, louder this time. "Yep, I'm a regular normal-phobic; gonna hafta write a book about that someday." He smiled at me briefly and slid the stone toward me so I could finish making his pizza.

I shook my head, laughing. A book about your best friend actually being an alien... from outer space. That's a great idea, if not a bit under done. "I wonder if that's the case for all of those alien books?"

Bryan shrugged. He rested his head on his hand and pulled his knees up to the edge of the counter, probably by tucking his feet on the shelf where they store the potatoes and onion. I finished the tomatoes and spread them evenly on the pizza and smiled; Bryan had to perfect the placement of every one of them.

Next, I picked up the bag of mushrooms that had been dumped from the paper bag and sliced and placed them on the dough, too.

"Why is it that when Mom makes this pizza it never tastes as good as when you make it?" Bryan had taken the cheese and started dressing the parts of the pizza that already had mushrooms.

I shrugged. "Maybe she doesn't use the correct amount of love. Mothers tend to use too much." I chuckled at the joke: Bryan's mom always bragged about how much love she puts into the food she makes for her family, me included.

Bryan cracked a smile, too. "So other than being weird, the new girl had nothing fun to say for herself?"

I lost my smile; he definitely had a way with conversations, never missing a subject change. "Well, she was pretty, and somewhat nice. She had a lot of... skin showing."

Bryan's eyes narrowed.

I gulped.

He did that kind of thing when he realized I was hiding something. I wanted to shrink down and pretend I was a speck on the floor, but alien or not, I'm not capable of doing that. Technically, I'm not sure what being an alien means at the moment; not much is different.

"What did she really look like, or rather, what was it about her that has you biting your tongue?" He leaned across the island just as we finished dressing the pizza; it was fully clothed and ready for a hot date, so I placed it in the oven.

"Well, she had really tight jeans, like... see-every-curve jeans; and she had a short shirt so I could see her belly button and everything in the middrift; and she had on a... a-"

9

Bryan leaned back again and breathed out relieved. "So, you like her. What's the big deal about that?"

I felt uncomfortable. My shorts felt like they had ridden up and were threatening to give me a wedgie and my sleeves felt constricting. "What if she's, you know, the one?"

Bryan burst out laughing. "The one?!? What's got you thinking like that? You've got to be joking."

I wanted to hit him or maybe kick him in the groin. He was being really immature about this, but that would be an empty accusation if I followed through of the previous urges.

So... I settled for pouting like a little kid that didn't get money for the ice cream truck.

"No, I just want to be prepared for that situation if it were to happen."

"More like you are interested in a girl you just met for the first time." Bryan kept laughing at my discontent.

"No, it's not."

"Sure it is."

"No, not according to my box of gadgets!" I crossed my arms and waited for a reply, but none came. I slowly turned to face Bryan completely.

His face no longer held mocking or jest, instead every cavity and nook was filed with concern. "It's about that?"

I nodded. I hadn't expected him to turn suddenly cold. I had expected him to still be rampaging on and on about the new girl, but his brain worked differently than most. Or maybe, it's just because I'm an alien, and maybe my brain is the different one?

"Oh, I'm... well, uh, what happened?" Bryan seemed to have sobered completely.

I turned and leaned my butt against the handle of the stove. I enjoyed doing that because it proved just how much I had grown over the last year and a half. "A gadget in the corner flashed a holographic-thing: it was the words, 'Match Detected'.

Bryan nodded.

"I figure it must be the new girl; she is the only *new* thing in town.

Bryan seemed to have sailed away. Or taken off. Whichever it was that he did when he had that far away look. "Did your mom have anything to say?"

I shook my head. My mother is an alien fanatic. She has pictures of when my *birth* mother left me, but she was traded a sample of DNA if she would keep quiet about it. I was really little, but my mom says that my *birth* mother said that I would remember it when the time was right... well, the time has never been right, so I still have no idea what is going on or why I'm here.

"Well, are you going to ask her?"

I wagged my head indecisively. My mom would probably think that it was another alien in town, or that I had to find it before a certain date or the world would end or some other insane theory. I love my mom, trust me, I do, but she can be a bit over the top at times, especially *alien* times.

My mouth felt dry, so I was relieved when Bryan decided to speak again. "Well, enough is enough. We can talk about this again later. Let's go pick out a movie to watch; it's already 7:00."

I cleared my throat, and without looking at a clock, I corrected him. "You mean 7:04."

We settled for a movie about a girl that wanted to rule her school and have a new club and finally ends up with the boy of her dreams. Yeah, weird pick for two teenage boys... well, that's because Bryan's sister Dani had barged in and hogged the TV with her friend Marissa. This also helped get rid of the whole alien business for a bit longer. I wanted to make sure my answers were acceptable. That meant I needed to think.

I used the setup of the movie to gather my thoughts about the new girl. Then, I used the conflict to map the different ways that the conversation could go.

I paid attention to the kiss; mostly because Marissa and Dani started squealing and I couldn't think straight while they were make the noise. But, then it was onto the climax; which gave me enough time to keep mapping the routes of our conversation.

That is about when my brain started going downhill. My brain started skipping down a path of the map I was creating that I hadn't anticipated. I chanced a glance at Bryan before I explored it a bit further. It somehow went from him and I fighting about whether I should pursue the new girl or not- I was going crazy because I didn't know her name and I refused to call her 'Black Thong' - but the fight turned into him confessing that he didn't like the idea of losing me to some girl, and then it got extremely weird.

I kissed him, in my head... I kissed him.

I quickly shook all of those thoughts out of my head onto the floor and rolled the dog so that it's back crushed the thoughts into oblivion. I turned to Bryan, who seemed to be falling asleep.

I wouldn't mind, I realized. Bryan doesn't have that bad of a personality, other than his big mouth about things that are relatively unimportant. He's tall, not something that I would discourage from a romantic interest. I was starting to warm up to the idea of Bryan. I know, a scary thought.

Then another squeal indicated the end of the movie. Marissa and Dani giggled and squeaked and

13

did other things that twelve-year-old girls do at the end of a romantic comedy that the 'Hottest Man, Survive according to *Teen Spot Mag*' kisses the 'Trendiest Girl according to *Hot Times Teen Mag*.

I then had a jarring realization: I am a guy.

A guy... liking another guy.

An *alien*, not of this world... liking a very human, suddenly very appealing, guy.

I am *Bi*? Isn't it bad enough that I'm an alien? Now I'm a homosexual alien. Maybe, I just admire him as a friend?

Tingles started in regions I wouldn't even admit in my mind. No, I'm homosexual. Maybe my race is homosexual?

Oh, gosh, now he's talking and I have no clue what he's been saying.

"So, what movie is it that you want to watch?" Bryan shifted on the end of the sofa until his butt was sticking up in the air and the majority of his upper half was in an awkward pose over the side of the arm reaching toward the DVD cabinet.

I was stunned, but not so stunned that I couldn't recite a bunch of lines from my favorite movie with my best friend. "That one!" I point like a maniac at the DVD cabinet, not even caring that I had no clue where on the cabinet it was. He knew what one I was talking about, and that's all that mattered.

14

Well, other than the whole homosexual alien thing... but I could deal with that later.

We watched my favorite movie of all time. Yes, and it was his favorite movie of all time too. I would tell you, but I don't remember what it was, mostly because I was preoccupied with Bryan at the time. He had shifted closer to me, but we were still on separate couch cushions. I was amused by the fact that I could practically sense how close he was, but also... I tried to remember if the feeling had always been there.

"You enjoying the movie?" I didn't even know what part we were at, but I had to think of an answer as quickly as possible.

I nodded. "I always do." I shifted and now my shorts really were giving me a wedgie, but I refused to fix them.

The best part came on screen and I started chewing on the tip of my thumb. Bryan clenched his entire body and I felt as the room between us increased until the end of the chase scene and he cheered. I cheered too, mostly because he did and I wanted to be like him: Human.

When he resettled onto the sofa for the end, I found that he was sitting almost flush against my side. My face must have been as red at the tomatoes I had put on the pizza earlier. Thinking of the Pizza earlier, made me think of him getting down the tray for me and being taller than me and being so close and showing concern with his entire face and then some... and that train of thought led to trouble.

So... I followed it.

Well, I tried to but then his hand came to rest on my knee and I had trouble following anything.

I swallowed.

I was about to turn into mush, and my brain was going to be nothing more than another experiment of human and alien interaction. Fatal. I breathed, defeated. I smiled though, I had a match... maybe that girl could help me to forget about the confused thoughts I kept having about Bryan.

CHAPTER TWO

That night, I had the weirdest dream: I ended up liking it, then it turned all around again and I wound up having no clue how to feel about it.

Bryan cheered for the chase scene and I giggled at his way of being immature; but then I joined cheering, too. He gave me a small smile that touched my heart, grabbed it and squeezed it repeatedly, making it pump faster.

He sat down next to me and slung his arm over my shoulder. I snuggled closer to him, resting my head on his chest and sniffing an intoxicating smell.

"Hey, baby, what's with you, you're awfully quiet?" I almost choked at the sound of his voice: It was deep and scruffy and absolutely irresistible. I felt like I should run, but also that I didn't have control of my body. His hand found its way onto my knee and he started sliding it up my thigh.

As much as I told this person to run, they wouldn't move... not an inch. Scratch that; this person moved several inches, in the wrong direction! Bryan's face and my face were not even an inch apart, but I didn't feel as awkward about it as I could have.

Then he kissed me.

And, it was wonderful.

I didn't fight the body I was in anymore. Instead, I let the body and then Bryan take the lead and do whatever they wanted. I felt blissful, as if the world were allowing me this one chance to test out my dreams, and so I did.

Until I was forced out of my dream.

Bryan had started to lean me back onto the couch, but I still didn't much care. The problem was when his hand started climbing up my shirt and tingles started forming in my chest and nether-regions. That was when I was jolted awake.

I was panting, covered in sweat and wishing that there was an explanation. From God, from mom, from my birth mom, from Bryan, from myself. I didn't care where it came from; what mattered was that I got it.

I was thirsty. It seems making out in your sleep makes your tongue feel like desert sand and your gums sandpaper and your teeth sawdust. I trudged into the kitchen from where I had crashed on Bryan's couch- didn't I tell you I would end up spending the night?

I reached up to get a glass from a shelf, but not a too-high shelf; then filled it with water from the filtered tap. That was the moment I realized something was off.

I looked out the window and could see the ghost of my reflection, something was wrong with it. I gulped down the water and put the glass on the counter before scurrying to the bathroom. I flipped the light switch and winced at the fluorescent lights. I slowly walked up to the mirror and jumped at my reflection: My chest was puffed out a bit and my hips were wider. My eyes seemed bigger and my eyebrows were thinner. I studied myself for a good three minutes before deciding it was all a dream.

I turned out the light and headed back to the couch. I lay down and stared at the ceiling while contemplating how to go about waking up. I decided on closing my eyes and going to sleep. But before I did, I had to do one thing. I ran my hands up under my shirt, up toward my chest.

I realized quickly, that it was not the same as when, in an earlier dream, Bryan had done it.

It just wasn't as fun.

CHAPTER THREE

The morning came sooner than I wanted it to. Dani brought a pillow to my face just as my eyes began to open. "Wake up, crazy boy!" I glared at her and turned over. "It's Monday," the pillow again, "you have," and again, "to go," and again, "to school," and again, "today!"

That last time hit woke me up. I hadn't noticed that yesterday was Sunday; I strongly believed that it had been Saturday. Only then in retrospect did I remember my Mom sliding the idea of church off of her mind because she thought she was on the brink of discovery... hence my confusion. I rolled off the couch and popped up off of the floor faster than I thought any sleepy person could, but I wasn't a usual person.

I grabbed my clothes and ran out of the house. I faintly heard Dani laughing and Bryan's mom shouting in the background that I wasn't wearing real clothes, but I wasn't sure if 'real clothes' would change the fact that I would be late or not to school. I ran past the new girl's house in time for her to close the door behind her and see me fly past in my pajamas.

She seemed surprised but then just turned around and walked back into her house.

I shook my head at myself and probably at my small town home. I really wanted to just leave but then what would my mother do? I was the DNA sample that was exchanged for her to be quiet. Would she show off her pictures and other evidence? Would I be hunted down? Would my birth parents care?

Oh, well.

I vaulted to the top of the front steps and threw open the door - my mother probably hadn't locked it since the night before. I ran up to my room and threw my gym bag onto the bed and changed in a hurry.

What would the new girl think of my clothes? Should I wear my blue t-shirt? I'm told it brings out my eyes. Would it look too planned out if I wore my blue sneakers with my blue T-shirt? Would I get noticed? It is a small town. Would the new girl care? Would Bryan care? Would Bryan like it better if I wore orange, since it's his favorite color.

I found myself thoroughly surprised that I was more worried about whether Bryan would like it than the new girl. That made me both distressed and bothered. But through all of my frustration, I felt a warm bubbling sensation in the pit of my stomach and a tingling in places there should be no tingling during normal everyday activities, like changing clothes and thinking of the preferences of your best friends.

But normal is for humans. And, I'm not human.

The tingling though did not stop at a simple tingling. No it turned into a swirling and aching and churning that was not comfortable. I felt dizzy and I fell back onto my bed.

"MOM!"

I turned to my side and held my knees to my chest. My head started tingling and my toes and fingers started spasming. I hoped she had heard me because I felt that if I yelled again the ringing in my ears would drone it out.

A presence entered the room and a quick glance told me it was my mom. She had on her science goggles and her white lab coat and even her sandy hair was rolled into a crazy style on her head. Nothing about my mom was normal; I liked it that way.

She sat on the bed and ran her hand down my spine, like she had when I was little and couldn't go to sleep. "Shhh." She ran her fingers in a light circle. "Don't worry."

If I could have spoken through this problem I would have screamed at her. Don't Worry? I'm dying, or in labor, or imploding.

The churning eased and I let go of my knees. I rolled back onto my bed and felt utterly exhausted mentally, but energized in every other way.

My mom smiled down at me. I wanted to wipe the quirky smirk off her face, maybe even bury myself in the ground and pretend I had never existed.

"It's the right time now." She said. "I'll tell you why you came."

I knit my eyebrows together in a fancy pearl stitch then stretched to a straight stitch, then I took a mental pair of scissors and scissed them apart into a expression of disbelief. She knew why I was here, but never had the inclination to tell me? I felt cheated.

"What?" Not exactly what I planned to say. I had planned on something louder and more rampaging in nature but this got the same point across.

"Your planet is dying." I shook my head in disbelief, not because I was from a dying planet, but because she really knew why I was here. "You were sent here to help repopulate the planet, when the time came. And... if worse came to worst, just to make sure that the DNA doesn't die out."

I sat up. I felt like the churning part of my stomach was being tugged in all directions.

"You needed to find a suitable partner. Someone who would contribute the correct kind of DNA that would further your race rather than destroy the last of the DNA. Your mate will have to harbor almost an entire set of recessive genes." She looked over to my closet. "Ever since you turned nine I have checked that box to see if the 'correlator', as your birth mother explained it, had found someone. I was happy when I came up this morning to see that it had, but also frightened to see that you weren't here." Almost as an afterthought she added. "Where were you?"

"Bryan's." That was all I could choke out.

She nodded. "I was hoping that you would know who your match is." She waited a moment.

I tried to speak, but nothing would come out. I wanted to say the new girl, but saying that would make me feel like she was the only one for me.

Mom must have realized that I was unable to speak so she continued. "I have been working on the antidote for the pandemic sweeping across your home planet. I think I've found it, but I can't be sure for a few more days time."

I cleared my throat. 'What was happening to me? You know, the aching and swirling and paining and churning and... premature death?"

Mom just nodded and nodded some more. She shifted the goggles further up her nose. "You were

24

chosen to spread your DNA for a reason, Kevin."
She put a hand on my shoulder. "You've finally
come of age... I started my period at 11, but, I guess,
all species are different."

I was thoroughly confused now. "Mom, I'm a
guy."

"You can change sexes. You can mate with
absolutely anyone of this planet with human DNA."
She smiled brightly; I felt that it was in complete
contradiction to the information she had just passed
on to me.

My throat was dry and my eyes felt spicy. I
seriously was going to bury myself and pretend that
I had never existed. I needed a shovel and a coffin
and maybe a sleeping pill that would keep me out
until after I had ran out of air, but who knows if that
would actually kill me or not?

"It won't hurt as much next time." She stood up
from my bed and walked toward the door. Before
she left, she turned and blew a kiss toward my
cheek. As much as I didn't want either the
statement or the kiss to reassure me, they did.

I felt seriously lost and like I didn't fit in.

Sure, all my life I had been hiding in a small town.

Sure, all my life I had been an alien.

Sure, all my life I hadn't a clue.

But now, I was the least bit human I had ever
been.

CHAPTER FOUR

I arrived at school just as the second bell rang. That meant that I had missed biology class. That didn't mean much to me; biology wasn't something the world wanted an alien to know. The world figured that aliens worked all that out through probes and tests and experiments. But, I had just picked up a textbook like everyone else.

I walked into English class and felt a small hint of frustration in my doubly exhausted brain. Bryan was scooting uncomfortably away from the New Girl who was sitting in my usual seat. She was leaning over to him, seemingly asking a question, but her lips weren't moving the way a talking person's would. Instead, they were making kissy moves at him.

Bryan's face turned a deep crimson color and he turned away from her and also away from me, who he hadn't seemed to notice. I felt hurt because he hadn't noticed me.

I trudged to the back of the room and sat in the seat catty-corner from the New Girl, the opposite way from Bryan.

She started to tease him about his hair. "So, a red head. A red head doesn't have a soul. You know that right?" Then she laughed.

I wanted to crush her head between my two bare hands, but that would leave too many fingerprints. I happened to admire his hair. I wish mine were like his, colorful; instead, I'm as dreary as a dessert under storm clouds with a forecast devoid of rain.

I stared down at my orange shirt. I was frustrated that I hadn't been able to sit next to Bryan. He would have complimented me and told me that he thought it was the best color in the world. Sometimes, I wonder if it's his favorite because his hair is another shade of it.

The New Girl shifted in her seat and a substitute teacher entered the room. The New girl's pants were so low, it looked like her butt was rubbing all over my chair. The one that is next to Bryan, MY chair. She propped her head on her hand and waited through roll call.

Bryan's name. "Here." He raised his hand. It showed off the length of his arm and the way that he was the tallest in the English class.

My name. "Present." I raised my hand. I chuckled as the New Girl sent me a nasty look. 'Match' or not, I liked ticking her off. Bryan's expression caught me in the headlights. His face looked so relieved that his mother could have died and he would have been sedated. Not that I wish that on his mother, she is a wonderful woman... when she isn't shouting about the benefits of real clothes over pajamas. I decided to look back at the New Girl, so that I wouldn't do something stupid. That stupid thing being an increasing tingling sensation everywhere in my body that vanished at the look of her face.

"Stormy Grace Wong."

The new girl put her hand in the air. "Alive." That earned a few giggles in the room and a glare from the sub.

I shook my head with disdain and avoided Bryan's eyes.

Our assignment was to write a poem. Mine so far?

'That's Stormy Grace;
        she's got one stupid face.
Yep, Ms. Wong;
        with the midnight thong.'

I don't think that I could turn that into my teacher... let alone a substitute that has proven that she hates kids and everything about kids, and probably school, and parents, and all life of THIS EARTH! Well, at least I was partially excepted from that.

Stormy seemed to be having a lot of fun putting her hands on Bryan, but I wasn't sure what to do about it. Part of the class, I spent glaring at her back in a confused manner and the other half, I spent trying to aim my paper airplane at the back of her head. I finished my poem. It wasn't the best poem but it would do. I felt like it left out details that I couldn't put in, so it was incomplete.

     When sitting and staring, you feel sorta rude
     Even though you know it is her attitude
     That is changing the way the world flexes and stretches
     And now you can see that the world's doomed to gloom
     Mostly because you're views are objective
     Because you don't fit in with the world around you.

My stomach finally quieted its churning enough to race to my next class, the only class that has assigned seats, so I couldn't sit next to Bryan.

I could hear Bryan's footsteps and knew he was probably trying to catch me so he could interrogate me about leaving his house without saying good bye and not being at Bio this morning. I didn't really want to talk to him though.

A seven block system is not very fun. You have every class, everyday, and you never get significant homework. Homework helps kids learn... or maybe I think that because I'm an alien. Different brain and all that.

Either way, I found myself staring at a white board filled with little black and blue lines. I think it looks more like a pale, abused man than a wall of math.

I couldn't avoid Bryan forever.

Lunch was a bit of a free for all. A small school has no need for separate lunches and, therefore, news spreads quickly. By lunch, the entire school knew that Stormy was a flirt. I was not in the mood for hearing about that though, so I headed to my friendly library and huddled in the biology nook.

I could hear the librarian munching on a biscotti that I knew was from Italy. Everyone knew that she was married to the millionaire author that was currently seeing people behind her back. Even she knew. But she liked real Italian biscotti, so she didn't leave him.

I pulled down a book and started reading about reproduction: "Every species has a different number of genes in their DNA, that it why we don't have weird hybrids like Centaurs or Anime Neko girls." I'm a mumbler, and I hate it. When I mumble the things I read, I can pay attention to them better but so can other people around me.

I was perfectly unaware of anything around me while I read -mumbled.

"Reproduction, huh? Is it nerd porn?"

I jumped. I even dropped the book and stared at the girl above me. Stormy's auburn hair looked grey and menacing because she was looking away from the fluorescent lights. She had her fists on her hips and a strand of hair from the front of her bobbed hair cut stuck in her mouth.

I picked up the book and replaced it on the shelf. "No, I was researching for a biology project."

She scoffed and spit the hair out of her mouth. "No, you weren't. I'm in your biology class. Red-head was looking for you when I took your seat. And we are not learning about reproduction, human or otherwise. Besides, animal reproduction is not very fun, all humping and barking and neighing"

I didn't think she meant the part about 'otherwise' to be an insult, but giving my current research, and position, it really did sting. "And you know a lot about this? Spending quality time with your animals?" I felt my eyes starting to water. I got up and moved toward the front of the library, and hopefully somewhere no one could find my body. I was having a lot of trouble dealing with her and my, for lack of a better word, 'period' at the same time.

31

She followed me though. "Did you just say what I think you just said?"

I swallowed. Her tone was not one of mere condescending but now of hurt slathered with anger. I was really hoping something would happen, either to distract her or put a wall of meat between the two of us. Lucky for me, I wasn't the only person she had rubbed the wrong way.

One of the largest guys in school. His name is Bill Harlequin, though most people call him Harley. He was a bully of sorts, taking peoples notebooks and flushing them down toilets. All of the teachers knew and even the parents knew, but no one wanted to say anything about it because his dad and aunt were not the kind to forgive people who had wronged their son.

I allowed him to butt in on my turn in mine and Stormy's conversation. "You going to say something else about being a nerd or are you going to be smart about what you do next?"

I didn't want to know how this would go. By now, she'd probably heard the rumors about Harley's family. Brother and a Sister and a Son; many people have insinuated things about that setup.

I slipped out of the library and walked down the hallway, hoping that I wouldn't run into anyone. My prayers were again answered and I got to the dark room without any trouble. I curled up in the back and cried for a bit, making sure no one knew I was there and silencing at the slightest sound to make sure that I wasn't found.

I swallowed and I started wishing that Bryan was there and able to tell me it was alright and that I shouldn't be crying. I didn't notice the tingling until it was too late. I felt my head tingle and hair start pushing out of my skull at an intermediate rate and I felt my chest tingle before blowing up like two small balloons. My eyebrows tingled and my lips tingled and my stomach and hips and waist tingled.

And I couldn't stop crying.

Some people think a small town is a great place to hide... well it isn't.

Finally, the 15-minute warning bell sounded and I wiped my face. I felt that my eyelashes were longer and my lips and cheeks were puffier. I started thinking about the girls I had seen in magazines. You know, those magazines filled with star-trash and Hollywood-sting. I had to be a boy before I got out of the dark room. It could be awkward walking up to Coach Crawford and saying that there must have been a mistake: I was a boy for 15 years and now I'm a girl.

Nothing happened though.

I tried a different magazine.

And another.

And then I started to worry.

My next and final class was PE/Health. Each was 45 minutes and you did them in your PE uniform. I have a *male* uniform.

I grabbed my backpack and turned the cylindrical door to leave the dark room. I looked around, panicking. I noticed the art closet and remembered that we had the winter play coming up, which meant we had clothes in the closet.

I stepped forward into the closet and looked around. Most of the stuff looked too much like a costume: A polar bear; a steam engine; a daisy. I started to wonder what play the school was putting on. For a small town, it is surprising how well they keep the play a secret. And they do. Right up until opening night.

In the back, there was a hanger with a black and white striped tunic and a black skirt. I grabbed them both and locked the closet door. I pulled off the orange shirt and tried not to be interested in my chest. It was really hard not to look around this new body. It was quite attractive, even if it was my own opinion.

I tried to pull on the top but it didn't fit. My new boobs were too big, so I ended up putting the orange t-shirt back on. The black skirt fit but it felt weird having so much leg showing. I also realized that during the transformation, my leg hair had disappeared and left my legs hair-free and silky-smooth.

It then struck me that I would need a bra or something. I looked around the costumes again and found a mermaid. Now, I really started to wonder about the storyline of this play. The mermaid costume had a bikini top, so I pulled that from its hanger. I put that on under my shirt and suddenly felt increased respect for females everywhere.

I looked down at myself and nodded silently before exiting the closet and heading to the locker rooms. I paused a second before opening the door to the left with a little blocky picture of a woman on it. I stepped in carefully and tiptoed to a mirror. I was immediately struck with a new problem: My hair.

It was long, very long; it ended at my elbows, except in the places where my boobs got in the way. But the biggest problem was the fact that from root to tail it was deep purple. It was pretty and my eyebrows had changed to match it, but in a small town, people don't overlook things like that.

I concocted a cover story of a laundr-o-mat and bleach and some ridiculously placed purple dye and a mother that decided to make it all match instead of it being splotchy.

I shuffled into the locker room. I didn't know what to expect, but what I saw wasn't what the guys next door ever fantasized. The girls were either waiting in line for a bathroom stall or they were shedding their skirts and tops to reveal the uniform underneath.

I was a little bit disappointed.

I trudged over to a line of lockers. There was a girl at the end; she wasn't the type of girl that the boys would fight over. She had on a baggy T-shirt and large glasses.

I tapped her on the shoulder, carefully. "Hey, do you have a uniform I could borrow?"

She turned and looked at me for a moment before nodding. Her glasses bounced on her nose enough for her to push them back up near her eyes. She pulled a pair of shorts and a yellow t-shirt from the top of her locker. I smiled and turned to set my backpack on the bench.

I shifted over a few lockers and started to pull off my shirt. Three different girls gasped and giggled. I looked over at them then down at my bikini top. I snarled at them. "My bras are in the wash."

They nodded then turned back to the line they were waiting in.

The girl I had borrowed the uniform from closed her locker and started to peel her shirt off. She had been in a few of my classes, but none this year, and I am horrible at names. I always thought she was a bit chubby; I mean she swam in her shirt and I figured it hid a pudgy body.

But my jaw must have hit the floor.

She pulled off the shirt and revealed, albeit not a thin body, but definitely not a glomptuous one. It was a pudgy, in a good way, figure. I pulled on my yellow t-shirt to hide the small blush that was invading my face.

"They weren't giggling at your bikini." She said absent mindedly with the shirt covering her face.

I pulled the shorts on under my skirt and then shed the skirt, too. "Really?"

She nodded. "Yeah, they were laughing at your belly button."

"What?"

"The new thing is all about belly button rings. If anyone doesn't have one, they aren't cool enough for dignity."

I shook my head then looked incredulously at the girls still in line. It was probably something they got from a Teen Trash magazine. I smiled at the girl with the glasses. "I know that this isn't very good, but I don't remember your name."

She stopped what she was doing and looked over at me. "Have we met?"

I swallowed. I forgot that I wasn't really Kevin. "I figured I should remember it, I've seen you talking to people in the hallway." I breathed in relief, hopefully not noticeably.

She nodded. "Yeah, I guess. My name is Coral; I go by 'Cory' or 'Cor'."

I smiled at her; she even smiled back. By then we were completely ready for gym. She even gestured for me to put my things in her locker. She must have thought I'd forgotten the key to my lock or something. "Can I call you Coral? I like it. My name is... Katerina. Some people call me 'Kat' but I prefer full names."

"Coral's fine. People usually don't use full names."

I nodded before we walked out of the locker room together and into the gym.

"Can I ask you something?" She was looking at me funny. "Why is your hair that color?"

I flicked my eyes upward toward my bangs. "Oh, that. Long story short. I had an accident with bleach and knocked into someone with purple clothing dye. It was white and splotchy and my mother figured to at least make it all match. Ding~ dong~, it was purple."

She laughed.

We joined the boys near the bleachers. I noticed Bryan looking around the room, jittering. He kept swaying side to side. A boy named Michael patted him on the shoulder and I was surprised by how high he jumped. "That's Bryan Newman. He's been having a rough day. Some girl in his classes keeps bugging him about his best friend."

"What do you mean?"

Coral was taller than me, too. Not as tall as Bryan, but I had a feeling that as a girl, I had shrunk. "I mean, as long as we keep it between us, I think he's gay. The New Girl, Stormy Grace, must have noticed something to think the same way. She's been asking him about this other boy name Kevin all day."

"But why? I mean, what makes her think that he likes this Kevin?"

I was blushing but I think that Coral passed it off as being caused by the subject matter itself.

She shook her head. "You should see the two of them together. They have a type of chemistry anyone could search for, forever, and never find." She paused for a minute before turning to look at me more fully. "The few times I've talked to them, Kevin was pretty nice to me. Kevin goes on and on about Bryan and Bryan talks about Kevin and the food Kevin makes." She nodded.

I smiled. "Well then, I hope they figure it out."

"Me, too. Stormy has done nothing but go on and on about it. I feel sorry for them both."

I watched as Bryan jumped at a few other people. "Well, let's go talk to him. He seems to need a friend."

We started walking toward him. I felt awkward with my boobs moving while I walked. I also wasn't sure if all girls got the aches in their back or just some. Coral followed, looking at the people we passed with a sort of curiosity. I stopped when we stood about 3 feet behind him. "Heya."

At first he didn't turn around, but after a moment of deliberation he did. "Hi?"

Coral smiled and waved. "Hey, you look like you need a friend."

Bryan nodded and gave her a small smile. My chest clenched and I felt an urge to touch his face. I smothered it and released it in a forced breath. "I'm Katerina. What's grated your nerve to dust?"

He scoffed. "Probably an industrial-strength cheese grater."

I smiled and Coral's face scrunched up. I tipped my head to one side to look at her confused. She shrugged to herself and looked around the room.

I turned back to Bryan. "You have a problem with all people or only those that touch you?"

Bryan opened his mouth then stopped himself. I searched his face for a moment. "Sorry, uh... you're not someone I know. When did you come to town?"

I shrugged, more like buying time to think of a good excuse. "Recently. My mom and dad are relocating, so I'm here with extended family until that's settled." Some of that could soft of be true...in a far-fetched way.

He nodded and Coral did too, but hers was more absentminded than his.

Coach Crawford walked in with a determined look on his face. "Everybody outside. We're walking the track since the Boy Scouts are using the gym tonight."

Everyone groaned. Me included. Coral again gave me a confused look. I covered quickly. "At my old school, if the Boy Scouts needed a room they would spend the entire afternoon setting up, disrupting everyone and everything in their way."

Bryan nodded. "Same here."

I smiled and followed him and Coral out to the track. I grabbed at my hair and flipped it over my shoulder.

I had to be careful. One wrong word and I was a goner.

In a small town, where everyone would hear.

CHAPTER FIVE

After school, I booked it home. Bryan took the same way, so I was scared he might catch up with me. I even took the short cut through the Millers' yard - and the Millers hate people cutting through their yard. If you touch it, they lodge a formal complaint to the civic league and they yell at you and stare at you funny at church. After a few days, you just constantly feel like someone is watching you. They deny it, but all the kids say the same thing. It feels like someone is always looking over their shoulder... well, except for me.

I opened the front door of the house and for the first time, ever, that I could remember, I locked the door. I breathed heavily and leaned against the door, hoping that the world wasn't completely against me, because that's what it felt like.

I left my backpack next to the door and walked to the stairs that led down to the laboratory. I counted the steps to the basement, mostly because if I didn't, I felt that I would cry. I pushed the curtain at the bottom to the side so I could enter.

The basement was all white, except for the low ceiling; it was painted with black chalkboard paint, and covered in white chalk spread into different equations and numerical patterns. I wasn't able to remember the last time I had been down in the basement, but since then, the counters along the edge of the room had been filled with articles and print outs on alien encounters and sightings. I picked up one from the closest pile and read the first few lines. It described grey creatures with thin arms and large heads. I looked down at myself. I looked nothing like that, but then I thought about the fact that I saw boobs and long purple hair and smaller feet, and realized that the article might be true. Perhaps my entire race could shapeshift or something.

I walked around the different islands with different paused experiments on them. I didn't expect my mom to notice me immediately but I also didn't think she would notice so quickly.

She looked up from her work. After a second of delay she walked over and wrapped me up in a big hug.

I was surprised she didn't ask who I was; I didn't look much like myself. "Do you hug all strangers that wander into your house?"

She shook her head and stepped back, removing her arms from around my shoulders. She lifted her goggles from her eye sockets. She had tears forming in her eyes and I felt awkward standing before her.

I had never liked to witness people cry.

She swallowed. "You look like your mother."

I stood for a moment, deciding whether or not I liked that news or not. I had never met the woman that had been my birth mother. I had an urge, an uncontrollable one to cry, to run to my room and lock the door.

I said it was uncontrollable, so I followed it.

I found myself lying on my bed staring at the ceiling. I was sort of wishing that my mom would follow me, but was relieved when she didn't. I really wanted to blend into the bed and lay there forever.

I wished something would make sense. Anything. If it did, I promised I would thank the whole world but no epiphany came to me. I felt like the stereotypical teenage girl. At least, what everyone was led to believe who read *Teen Trash*.

It wasn't long before my self-pitying was interrupted by a knock on the front door. I popped off the bed and bounced down the stairs. I have a weird obsession with mail and packages; I have to be the person to pick them up or sign for them or look through the letters. I have always had a weird attachment with letters and cards; I have kept every card that I received in the mail from friends, pen pals, and family.

In fact, when I was little, my mom signed me up for a pen pal group at the now dilapidated and unused, community center. She would drop me off every Saturday for two hours to write a letter to a kid on the other side of the world. One day she came in before the end of the class; customarily she had been late due to forgetting me there because of the work she did in the basement. She walked in and saw that I had an entire stack of letters ready to be mailed. This wouldn't have been a problem except that I was in 1st grade and I had only just started to learn how to write sentences. She looked over a few and decided I wasn't allowed to go anymore because it was raising suspicion. I had written a dozen letters with words like 'sincerely' and 'gargantuan' in the time it took for the other kids my age took to write one.

On the way home, she had asked me why I felt I had to write so many. I answered with a simple fact. "I like getting letters." She laughed. But I never went to the class again.

I skidded in front of the door with the handle grasped firmly in my hand. I snuck a look out the window and saw a full head of bright red hair.

The handle became molten lava, hot in my hand. I let go because of the sudden burn. I looked down at my chest and then upward at my hair.

I ducked to the side, thanking god for Bryan looking in the opposite direction. It was a life saver.

I breathed heavily and different trains of thought rushed through the station without stopping. I couldn't board one long enough to get anywhere.

I was happily surprised when my mother poked her head from the staircase to the lab. She raised her eyebrows at me and then flicked her eyes to the door. This was the first time I had ever understood the body language my mother used. Maybe it was because I was finally a female. I was happy we didn't need to use words because our walls were thin and even when it was just a friendly neighbor, I could still hear the rude remarks about the house and the crazy lady that lived there from the other side of the door.

Mom walked toward the door and peeked out through the window. She nodded.

She shoved my shoulder to the side while the other hand opened the door.

"Yes? Oh, hello, Bryan."

"Oh, yeah, is... is Kevin home?"

"No, I thought he was with you." She shifted her feet. "He's not with you?"

I would've given anything to see Bryan or at least peek at his face. I would give even more to talk to him. "I thought he must've left school early; he wasn't in gym today."

Mom nodded, thinking. "Well, I'll have to be off looking for him."

"Can you tell him that I need to talk to him? Tell him it's about the new girl?"

Mom looked straight out the door, probably at Bryan. "Oh, that's right, the new girl. Is she nice?"

I knew after the door closed, the new girl would be our new topic of discussion.

"She's been driving me crazy; I didn't get to sit next to Kevin at all today. She would always take that usual seat." There was a shuffle outside. It must have been Bryan scuffing his shoes along the porch. "I just, I just need to talk to Kevin. Tell him I was here."

Mom waved. "Alright. I'll see you later."

"Yep. Bye, Ms. Z."

Mom closed the door and seemed to contemplate locking the door or not before locking it. That was also the first time I had ever seen *her* lock the door.

She turned to me; I was plastered against the wall, in the bikini top and the skirt from the artist closet. She gave me a look that I, suddenly being a girl, understood as 'Now, do-you-mind-telling-me-what-that-was-about'.

I smiled sheepishly.

Small town, even smaller home. I smiled wider.

I didn't never remember the last time my mother and I had sat down for dinner together and ate and talked. I tried not to think that it was because she had always wanted a daughter. But I will say that as a girl, it takes a steamboat to stop your mouth from talking.

I told mom about Stormy and my first poem, to which her only reply came as, "I like that poem. I would've turned it in just to see the look on the teacher's face. Of course, that is probably why I got C's in school."

I told her about the 'animal porn' incident. I have to say, I love my mother. "I think people should discipline the kid but start leaving that family alone. They are only the way they are because they have been under scrutiny ever since the kid was born." She got up and put the kettle on to boil.

I told her about the clothes and the dark room. "I'll get you some clothes from the attic. I planned for this. Every time you grew I would buy three outfits in case you started." She said matter-of-factly. She, also, swung her finger in small circles praising herself for being prepared.

I shook my head, laughing to myself. After she sat back down, we ended up laughing together.

I told her about the looker room, including how it wasn't how any of the boys had ever thought. She tutted but we ended up laughing again.

I told her about Coral. She smiled. "Maybe she's your 'one'?"

I shook my head. "Coral had brunette hair; I don't think that's recessive."

Mom just grimaced. "You're right."

I sighed. "If I knew who it was, at least, I could romance them or get used to them, or whatever."

Mom shook her head. "It doesn't work that way." She got up and grabbed two mugs from the cupboard. She poured the water into the mugs and threw a packet of Swiss Miss in my direction. I read the front to make sure it was with marshmallows, another quirk of mine.

It was. I reveled at how well Mom knew me, even though our paths rarely crossed.

I leaned back and pulled out the silverware drawer and took out two spoons. I handed one to Mom.

"When the detection alarm sounds, a sort of timer starts counting down, and there are certain paths to take from that moment forward until the trial is over." She mixed her packet's contents into her water thoughtfully, recalling words told to her many years ago.

I scrunched up my face. "What?" I sipped at my hot cocoa. It was very hot, so I coughed and spluttered very un-Kevin-like. "Girlth mouthth are thenthiitive." I cupped my mouth.

Mom went on like nothing had happened. She pulled her goggles from her head and yanked her hair band out of her hair. "Well, when the alarm went off, it meant that two people were in the proximity that would be suitable. Both must have the almost full set of recessive genes. By the end of the time allotted, you must pick one."

"But I'm only sixteen. Am I supposed to fall in love and never break up with this person, ever?"

She shook her head. "Your species only falls in love once."

"But humans don't."

"I know; I'm getting to that." She blew on her cocoa then sipped at it. I mimicked her, finding that it helped. "From the moment you meet anyone with mostly recessive genes that is suitable to be your mate, you appeal to them. You may stop growing if they are fans of a shorter person. You may have a change in eye color because they like someone with that color of eye, but, before you ask, it changes nothing about you the person. Only your looks or you're knowledge of the things to make or give them. You're even equipped with a 'sixth sense', really just heightened empathy, but anyway, that helps you to know what they want."

I blinked a few times, maybe more than that. "So I look nothing like what I'm supposed to?"

Mom just shrugged. "It seems that whoever prefers your female side is new to town, since those looks are unchanged. But who knows about your male looks, they may have been changing ever since you were little."

"So, do you know anything more? Maybe what kind of things I give them or anything?" I was feeling lousy and I still had no clue who to blame.

"Like if you were to wrap a present, you would pick the right paper, and the fact it was from you would make them like it more. You also influence them a little. If they like it, that is. If they were to receive two identical things, they would like it more if it was the one you gave them. Even if you switched the boxes. Also, if they find out afterward that it wasn't actually you who gave them something or that you lied, they would be extremely irritated but also have an urge to get over it *instead* of over you and leave you."

I was feeling personally betrayed by myself. I stared at my hands in fear that they knew all of this and were doing things even when I didn't know it. "So, again, what kinds of things?"

"Anything."

I swallowed. I didn't want to think of *anything*; I wanted a precise answer. "Like..."

She swallowed. Her eyes twisted around in her skull; she knew something that I didn't. "Like birthday gifts and cards."

She got up abruptly; I was going to ask her 'where the heck is *she* was going'. But settled on

51

watching her leave. I felt drained. Like someone took everything I knew about myself and dumped it out of my skull, leaving me hollow and only the dewy residue of myself in my chair.

I coughed into my mug; it rippled the reflection that stared back at me. It wasn't really me. It was an alien with purple hair and bright green eyes; it was a mother I had never known. It was a side of myself I had never known. "What part of myself do I know?"

I spent the evening trying to do homework. I still stand by my statement that no one in the public school system gives out homework, so I take it upon myself to give myself homework. During any class, if I have a question, I write it down and then later research it until I get an answer.

I had many questions on my papers today; ranging from "What does a ! mean in math?" to "Why do humans naturally assemble into cliques?"

Most of my research went well until I found the last of my pages of notes. It was from Health class and it wasn't exactly the best questions for conventional research.

I scrunched my eyebrows together into a fuzzy ridge. Though, I guess, that wasn't entirely true; my eyebrows weren't the ones I was used to. They were plucked and trimmed and elegant, by no work of my own.

I flopped back on my bed and reread the question: Why would Coral think that Bryan likes me (Kevin)?

I thought about it. Nothing I had seen led me to that conclusion. He had always been a good friend, nothing out of the ordinary. Nothing *different*.

When we were little, I mean like two years old, we had played house and he had been the husband and I had been the wife but that was because we were little and didn't know what we were doing. But then again, I raised a hand up to my light and let the shadow fall across my eyes. I stared at the fingers. It was still weird to look at the female hand connected to my mind. The nails were purple, matching my hair, again by no work of my own.

These hands had been doing all kinds of things without me knowing. They had been giving people what they wanted for as long as I had known anyone. They were doing things without consulting me first.

My arm went suddenly slack. That was work of mine, though. I lay on my bed, looking up, feeling like my lie of a life wasn't my lie anymore. It was someone else's. A joke, an inside joke, that I wasn't even in on.

I flailed for a moment, my entire body flopping off the bed and back. I don't know why, maybe I thought it would make it more real, maybe it would prove it wasn't really my body.

Maybe my body had done things to people without me knowing, and maybe I couldn't have stopped it, but I still felt guilty. Maybe, just maybe, all those years with Bryan had affected him.

Maybe he wasn't really Bryan anymore, like how I wasn't me.

Maybe he wouldn't have stayed my friend.

I decided to make a pact with myself. No more Bryan. At least, not until I sorted all this out. I wouldn't really get to see him in this body anyway; he barely knows 'Katerina'.

I wrote it down. I also had to figure out what to do with all my notes. If I was to be the new kid, I would have to play the part.

I signed the bottom of the pledge and ripped it out of my notebook.

I stepped into the hall to ask my mom for money to go shopping but instead, almost tripped and broke my new nose. I looked down at the pile of stuff leading to the guest room. I followed the small trail and saw my mom hanging clothes in the closet.

"What are you doing?" I leaned against the door jam. I was definitely shorter as a girl.

"Just getting your room ready." She hung up more clothes. "Also, you'll need to return those tomorrow, so I'll try to wash them later. Remember to leave them on top of the laundry basket." I nodded soundly. She turned and added some more clothes.

"I thought you only had three sets of clothes."

She turned to me for a brief second. "I lied."

I shook my head, surprised that she even admitted it so willingly. "Let me help." I started to pick up a box but found I wasn't able to lift it. I decided to try again. "Damn it."

She clucked at me.

If only she knew the other words in my vocabulary I could have chosen.

Mom walked over and helped by lifting the other end of the box. It was still a struggle but we got it to the bed. I wiped my forehead. "Why was that so hard?"

"Because you're a girl... and not used to your body yet." She opened the box and started pulling out knick knacks and trinket-y things. She gingerly unwrapped each item and set it somewhere in the room. I joined her. I thought it was surreal unpacking things for *my* room that weren't *mine*.

When the room was done, Mom left me to get familiarized with the place. I was glad it wasn't pink. Pink would have been the death of me.

I poked at a music box that played some unknown song. I toyed with a stuffed chinchilla, the only plushie stuffed-animal mammal. The rest were aquatic; this led to the conclusion that they were once my mom's. I knew a lot about Mom. She had only a few pictures from what she called her 'past life' as a micro-marine-biologist, but I had seen every one of them.

At least, I thought I had.

"*I lied.*" I heard her say the words again in my head.

I wondered if there was anything else she'd lied about.

I stripped to my underwear, which was still tight boxers and a loose bikini top, and rummaged through the closet to find what I would wear to bed. I found a pair of long pale-green flannel bottoms and a plain white T-shirt. I wasn't entirely sure how I was supposed to wear them; with underwear, without? I settled on without and crawled into bed, looking around the room, trying to memorize it for the morning.

I was anxious about waking up. Like my mail obsession, I also had a waking-up obsession. I always woke up on the right side of the bed, as in 'opposite of left'; and I hated, absolutely hated, the feeling of being lost or out of place in the morning. Like when you wake up in a hotel after the first night and it feels like something is really wrong and you can't remember where you are or why you're there. Yeah, many days have I ended up staying home from school due to that feeling because it lingers until well past lunch and the only thing I can do is sit curled up and cry.

I closed my eyes and hoped I could fall asleep because it would be a very long night if I couldn't.

What must have been hours later, I fell asleep. Due to my alarm clock and my extreme sense of time, though, it had actually only been 10 minutes.

CHAPTER SIX

I woke up and felt right at home. I lazily rolled over to the other side of the bed and got up. This me, the female one, seemed to belong to the room just as the things started to belong to her. I stretched and opened the door to my closet. Inside, were many sets of clothes that appealed to me, unlike the day before.

I pulled out the first thing to catch my eye. It was purple and green and orange and yellow, all zig-zagged across a high rise skirt. The rest of the outfit matched the various colors in some respect, like the bright purple puffy-shouldered, half sweater.

Downstairs, my mother was back to wacky business-as-usual. She had left out two waffles for me. Who knew how long they had been there? So for the first time, and probably because I was female now, I made another set from the freezer and set the two on the plate into a bag to feed to the birds on the way to school.

Next to a new backpack were the clothes I had borrowed the day before. I slid them into the backpack and shuffled the books and papers around in the book bag; I couldn't let it look too new.

A note was taped to the top of my biology book.

Have a good day, darling. The Principal knows that you're a new kid and I used your current transcript to get you into the same classes. I also said you needed routine and that was how it was at your old school. Love, Mom.

I shook my head. She never before had left me a note or sent me off in the morning like this... at least not since 4th grade. I shrugged and picked up the back pack and left through the door.

The walk to school was longer with shorter legs. I also knew that Bryan would probably be on his way to my house to pick me up. Mom would cover for me though, just like yesterday.

School was suddenly new again. People were already muttering about the 'other new girl' - which was me. I trudged into the office at the front and asked for my schedule. The receptionist nodded and buzzed in to the Principle. After a moment, the computer blipped with a message and I was nodded in.

I wasn't sure if it was customary to get your schedule from the Principle herself or not, but by the looks I got, it must not have been. I felt like a snake in a terrarium; no one trusted me and they could mock me through the glass.

The heavy door took some coercion to open but it did after a silent argument. On the other side of the door was a large mahogany desk with a small plate of scones and a mug of tea. Neither looked at all touched. I got a funny feeling that I should take one, so as I sat down, I reached for one but stopped myself. I still felt like I should take one, but didn't dare.

The Principal walked through the door. Her shoulder brushing the heavy door lightly but opening it far enough that it bounced off the rubber stopper on the opposite wall. She was wearing a white and navy vertical-striped pinstripe suit. I thought that it looked well on her; it matched her dark hair and her slits for eyes. She was young, maybe twenty-two; I would've guessed lower if it weren't for the fact that she must've had her doctorate not to mention the other small million of certificates littering her office walls.

She set down her blackberry with a sigh. "I'll never understand this technology." She dropped a canvas bag on the floor before sitting in the oversized chair and leaning back to take a few deep breaths. "Yes?"

I wasn't sure if she was talking to me. I sat awkwardly waiting for some other recognition.

She opened one eye quickly. "Yes, you. What are you here for again?"

I swallowed. Her voice was thick and heavy, not like a man's but like cheesecake, elegant and rich. "I'm Katerina. This is my first day." I shifted my feet. They were in yellow and white baby doll flats, or at least, that's what my mom called them when we put them away.

"Are you sure?"

My head snapped back up; I didn't understanding her question. "Sorry?"

She peaked from under her eyelids again. "You were in my school yesterday. Want to explain that to me?"

I know I must have blushed by the amount of heat that flooded my face. I also had nothing to say, so I settled for biting my lip and jittering any appendage that I was aware of. My heart and intestines were probably jittering too.

She smiled lazily. "Nothing to say for yourself."

I was surprised by her tone; it wasn't a question like she knew something I didn't. She wasn't the only one. "I don't."

"That wasn't a question." I knew that but I still had to say something. I again almost reached for a scone. It was like my body thought it should but my brain was trying to smother it.

Then it could no longer be kept at bay and my hand sped forward before bring a scone just as quickly to my mouth, almost smashing it into my face at that speed. I got crumbs on the name plaque on the desk, though. I wiped it off: Dr. Lidiya Petrov. She sounded eastern European. But she looked like your everyday 'Jennifer Day'. My eyes flicked from the name to her again.

Her face split with a smirk. "More questions than answers, huh? I have a similar problem with you." She didn't have a Russian accent or anything, either.

I swallowed the chunk of scone in my mouth and my hand added another. I watched as she got up and sat on her desk and turned to me. "Anything you want to tell me?"

I shook my head.

"Are you absolutely sure?" I nodded. "What if I tell you that you can tell me anything, free of bias, free of tests or prejudice, and it will never leave this room."

My eyebrows came together in what I hoped was lady-like confusion.

"Kevin."

My eyes snapped up to her face. I wasn't sure if it was a joke or if she was talking about something else. But my reaction seemed to please her.

She sat back down in the chair. My hand stuffed another bite of scone down my throat. "Was that so hard? I don't want you to eat that anymore." My arm went limp and I felt relieved to swallow without choking on more. "You don't have to be scared, this town in full of 'em. At least, it used to be. Most either moved away or died out." She sunk back in the chair and took a deep breath. "Even me."

"What do you mean?" I coughed and she poured me a glass of water from a pitcher behind her somewhere.

"I'll show you because you won't believe me if I tell you." Her appearance started to melt away with every blink. Soon all that was left was a grizzly bear-sized bug. Well, something of the sort. It had three eyes and a clear exoskeleton. You could see the food digesting in her stomach and the blood, or whatever she had, flowing through her body, but not in veins, but more like the cytoplasm in a cell.

I wasn't sure if I could keep my breakfast, and more importantly the scone, in my own stomach. Biology was a scary thing; she looked like a living biopsy.

Then, again with every blink, though now I was blinking with a purpose, she started looking like the woman that had nudged the door open. She was hugging herself a little when she was completely returned. She breathed in and out a few times. "Can you do that?"

I shook my head. I didn't know for sure, but I didn't think I could.

"I didn't figure you could. You seem to be a 𝄖 ☹ 𝄞. They're probably the best species at mimicry I've ever come across."

I nodded, not knowing if I was dreaming or nightmaring or just crazy-ing. I took a deep breath and tried to right myself in the world again. "You said there are many of us?"

She nodded. "We have an AA meeting every Tuesday and Thursday. You should come."

"AA? Alcoholics Anonymous?"

She scoffed. "No, aliens Abandoned. But that explains the weird looks at the city council meetings."

"The city council knows?" I was thrown for another fruit loop.

"Only half. It's a law in the city founding documents. Half of the council must be of the 'otherwise tested'." She actually used air quotes. "This city was made as a haven for the extraterrestrial."

I heard a bell go off in my head. "It's 7:20, I have to get to class." I started to get up.

"Sit down!"

I smacked my butt back into the chair.

"I'll write you a pass if you need it." She swiveled her chair again. She smiled with a mischievous twinkle in her eye. "How old am I?"

I swallowed. "You're never supposed to guess a lady's weight or age."

"Ooh, good choice, but really, I'm asking you to guess."

I nodded. "I don't know, 22?" Might as well go with gut instinct, right? But my gut started to twist and a different number came to mind. "Wait. This is going to sound ridiculous but my mom says to go with my gut..." She looked at me with appraisal in her expression. "54."

After it left my mouth, I felt like an idiot. Now she would be frustrated with me and I'd be outted.

"Closest yet! Nice. I'm going on fifty-six." I openly gawked. "You've got good instincts."

"You mean 'second' gut feelings." I felt like I was still at fault for something. For not knowing there were other aliens, maybe? I guess it was pretty self-centered of me to think that I was the only one.

She shook her head. "The disguise is what you size up first but it takes a moment for your real gut instincts to step in and realize something is off. You did wonderfully."

CHAPTER SEVEN

My day wasn't much different than the one before. Glare at Stormy, get whispered about. Except that it was a girl's feelings being hurt instead of a boy's not-much-change. But I did realize some things I had never noticed before. Probably because I was hyper aware of other aliens now.

Harley had a weird way of eating. He would mush everything up first and once it entered his mouth, you could faintly hear a gurgling sound. Once, I even saw some greenish goo still draining at the back of his mouth when he opened up for another bite.

Gina, a girl in my math class, came in late and she had to sit in the last available seat, near a window. She pulled her white hoodie up and over her head and even pulled her fingers into the ends before she was able to sit down. She also pulled her socks up to cover her ankles where her pants weren't long enough to cover. She sat angled away from the window and I could see a slight redness across her nose where she had turned her head to shift in her seat.

Also, in front of Gina, was a boy named Simon who had been last to enter the room before the bell. He looked around before sitting in a seat on that side of the room. He was excused to get his water bottle filled three times without getting so much as a grumble from the teacher. And Mr. Jennings hated bathroom requests or otherwise, so I figured the teachers had to know, too.

I wrote down a new set of questions and observations in one of my new notebooks. I found it cool to notice these things. I was like a detective. Sherlock Holmes, or otherwise.

It wasn't until I went into the locker room that my day took a dive. I was scared that if I asked Coral for another pair of clothes it would look weird but she just winked and gave me another. I found out from her "Don't worry about it, you can keep your stuff in my locker, I know there are no more lockers available during this class." I gave a sideways glance to the obviously empty and unused lockers behind us. She then whispered, "Just say what they want to hear, they won't ask questions."

I figured that meant she was an alien, too, but nothing about her seemed off or out of the ordinary. I decided I would ask her later. We exited the locker room and waited for class to begin. We sat on the bleachers and talked about all sorts of things.

She talked to me about boys in general and lightly about girls. She seemed to be aware that too much talk was a bad thing and I gave her my silent 'thank you'. She also stayed as far from the subject of Bryan as we could. Even when we both noticed his entrance with two other boys; one was Michael, a dark-skinned boy who looked more purple than African American. I opened my mouth to ask but Coral beat me to it.

"Yes."

I exhaled.

The other boy was Dustin; he was just weird. I always thought it was drugs or alcohol, either used by his parents or himself. Everyone knew that his folks grew 'medicinal herbs', but maybe...

"No."

I looked over at Coral. I think I figured out what made her an alien. She must be able to read minds or something.

"Or something."

I glared at her.

"Sorry."

I shrugged. I was dumbfounded by how little I had noticed of all the little things. They obviously pointed to something peculiar. I hadn't even thought of it before. I shook my head to myself.

Coach Crawford entered from a set of double doors beside the bleachers. He knocked lightly on the seat Coral was on and gave a small smile to me. "Nice to know other aliens have gender problems." He chuckled while my brain tried to faint and blow up at the same time. "I'm both; the wife took a while to get used to it."

Coral laughed politely. "Now you're just going to scare her."

He nodded and walked toward the rest of the kids in the gym before announcing himself with a holler. "What'cha standing around for? Get a move on. Five laps outside before anything can happen!"

Coral and I trailed behind everyone else. Once outside, I turned to her. "You seem old." I cringed. "That came out wrong, I'm sorry. I meant, uh..."

She waved it off. "I'm pretty old. I'm nearing my 200th birthday, but I don't mind it. On my planet I would either be working in the fields or gathering sap. At 200, I would start to do the fueling. Trust me, Earth is a lovely place to be."

"Fields? Sap? Fuel?"

"We're a slave race." I watched her face closely. "Like horses or bees. Doing the menial things that the other beings don't want to do."

I walked a little slower. "Sorry."

"No, it's fine. At least here they are still mindless. Think of my species as horses that after years of evolution was able to communicate and think just like humans."

It was hard to imagine, honestly. So I gave up and decided that I would have to do more imagining later. "So, is 200 old? Is it young?"

She smiled. "I'm still a baby, but here I've got enough wisdom for many lifetimes."She laughed. "Honestly, if I were on my planet growing up, I would look like Shaquille O'Neal when I was finally an adult."

I stopped walking, to stare at her, through space. But I wasn't really looking at *her*, I was looking at the *space*. After a moment I shuffled hurriedly to catch up. "What?"

"When we are about 700, we are prime for mating with those that are in their 800s. At 800, our body goes through a gender switch, hermaphroditism, like blackspot angelfish. We go through the same thing. I would first grow larger in size and more muscular, then change gender, and to signify the end of my change, I would develop a different skin color. Then once we're male, we can become full members of society, going to school and working for compensation."

That ended my talking for a while; I had a lot to think about. Coral as an eight-foot black man. I couldn't get over the idea. I didn't even have to think the question for her to answer it.

"Yes, I live with two people that appear to be tall gay black men."

I nodded. Okay, I was starting to feel the 'nave'.

We've all got a secret and the town was keeping its mouth sealed.

It was a miracle.

I had done well to stay away from Bryan all day, but just because I could, I decided to sneak, as in like-a-ninja, up to the second floor of the school. Of the schools two floors, the second looked much newer than the first. The town had to build the second floor when it started filling in with more people. Being a suburb of Washington D.C., it had been a lot of growth in a little time.

I looked up at the door jamb of one of the two identical lab rooms. I liked the lab rooms; they made me feel at home.

We only had two because it was like the TV cart; the different teachers would rent the room during their class if they needed it for the lesson. Behind the door was a small army of voices. I recognized Gina's and Harley's but the rest sort of jumbled together.

I knocked.

Behind the door, the room became eerily quiet. But again, I could single out Harley's whine "We got another one?"

I chuckled to myself, though it was mostly breath.

The knob turned and I looked into the room. I could see Gina in her white hoodie, though she wasn't completely bundled up; I could see Coral sitting on a stool in front of everyone. Harley had on a medical mask covering his mouth and nose. I shot it a look. He shrugged, "Ran out of breath mints."

I peeked around the room. I also saw a girl that had dark pink hair and a few piercings and even a ring of eyeliner that was at least a quarter of an inch thick all the way around. She rolled her eyes. "It's all natural, humans get acne, I get black circles and spots and freckly things."

I nodded. I was glad she got that out of the way before I made a fool of myself. Coach Crawford sat in the back reading a book. Upon better inspection, I saw the title *So you thought you were a boy...* I was hoping it wasn't for me but then he looked up and shoved the book in my direction. I took it, trying not to really touch it.

Dr. Petrov sat at the desk looking through lists on the computer. She was still as human looking as ever. Michael sat with his eyes wide open; I could see the now-green-tinted eyeball around his black pupil and his skin was totally purple, no question. I guessed he must have shed his disguise, too.

I sat awkwardly next to Gina and faced everyone else. Coral smiled and turned her body toward me. "Now, stand up and introduce yourself and everything." She guestured with her hands that I should get up.

Coach Crawford opened his mouth to say something.

"Shut your mouth and sit down, you're here for the same reasons."

I winced. It seemed Coral was incharge of Earth's fleet of misfit toys.

"I'm Katerina- or Kevin- and I don't know what kind of alien I am... but humans don't change gender, so I'm not human." I hadn't stood up. The look Coral gave me was a little unnerving, like I had betrayed her trust by not doing as she's ordered.

"Hi, Kevin-Katerina." Gina was friendly and held out a hand. The hand, though, found a stray ray of sunlight and was quickly pulled back. "Sorry."

I shrugged. Harley thumped my back with an open hand and I almost fell over from the impact. Michael twitched and smiled. "Nice to have you here; something smelled about you from the beginning."

"I'm sorry?" That was more about the 'smelling' thing. I hadn't thought I had smelled. I sniffed my arm: It just smelled like watermelon and strawberries, like my shampoo.

Michael shook his head and gave a friendly grin. "Super smeller. You didn't smell human's all I'm saying." He reached over to shake hands and I took it. Only after did I realize that his alien form secreted some ungodly slime. I swallowed my stomach down a second time that day and shook his hand politely then let go. I refused to wipe it on my clothes and certainly wasn't going to ask for something to wipe it off with. "You're nice." Michael said, then handed me a towel.

I nodded thank you. "Just being polite."

Coral smiled. "Good, then. Anyone want to explain what we do in this group?"

Gina shook her head. Her midnight black curls bounced back and forth. The girl with the black spots glared at the board behind Coral. Dr. Petrov returned to the computer screen and started typing, ignoring the question.

Michael sighed. "It's not that bad really. We just keep the town's secret, well, a secret."

I felt my *feminine* eyebrows come together like dainty silk worms.

He elaborated. "The town was formed way back when the US was only a handful of colonies. It's kinda weird. It was so the government could control the aliens but not be too close, you know."

I waited a beat and a half before shaking my head 'no'. He shrugged.

Coral clapped and all the attention was back to her. "So-" She cut herself off with a glare that could kill even Dr. *Cockroach* Petrov. I was confused, like out of it, until there was a knock on the door, again. I turned slowly and up close and personally experienced the chill of opening the door

while everyone was out of the metaphysical —
metaphorical didn't cut it — closet.

This was all pretty, darn well, real.

The door creaked open and Simon walked in with
his water bottle and a shoulder bag. He waved.

Gina got up and walked over to him and hugged
him. "Nice to see you made it."

He smiled. "Well, my wonderful girlfriend told
me not to skip it for the robotics lab seminar."

Gina smiled, giddy and child-like.

Coral waved them in and Michael shot up to fill a
basin on the counter with water.

I pulled my feet closer to the chair legs and
wrapped my arms around my shoulders. So many
aliens; I was feeling so stupid for thinking I was
alone.

"So, what did I miss?" Simon sat in the chair
next to Gina and started to untie his shoelaces. Gina
smiled. They held hands and made sticky eyes at
eachother.

Michael set the basin of water at Simon's feet.
"Not much, just getting *Keverina* settled in." He sat
back in his seat and grinned at me.

Simon stuck one foot in the water basin and
started to untie the other shoe. "Oh, hi." He stuck
the other foot in the water, too. "Nice to meet you.
So, do you change sex often?"

He gave a pointed look at Coach Crawford. I giggled. "No, just on extra-special occassions."

Everyone smiled politely at me and I let go of my shoulders. I shook them out a little and took a deep breath.

They were all aliens too.

I really wasn't alone.

CHAPTER EIGHT

The meeting ended briskly and the smile on my face must have been big enough to fit an entire lab table. I learned some really cool things.

Gina and Simon emptied the basin of water. It turns out that he needs the water or he has extreme drying out, and that's why his family lives near the lake in a shack, because technically they live in the water itself.

Michael walked over to the lab closet and opened the door. I looked into the cabinet and froze. There was a human body hanging there, all deflated and eyeless and mouthless. I snapped my mouth closed. I liked my mouth.

Michael turned and glanced over me to someone. That someone cleared their throat and Michael looked toward me. He blushed a light green. "Sorry." He walked over to me.

My eyes were getting dry; I had forgotten how to blink. "Uh-yuh-ah." The most itellectual response of the day, note the sarcasm.

Michael smiled sheepishly. "It's called a Shimmer. I blinked.

"Like, you know, in Doctor Who?" Michael stared, hard, at me.

I blinked again, then nodded slowly.

77

"It helps me to blend in. You'll need to know all of this stuff at some point. I'll make you a disc or something, explain some things. That okay?"

I nodded. "Uh-yeah... yeah." I was starting to remember how to form words.

I waved my goodbyes and left, promising to be back the following week. Words were totally back and forming and dancing little dances like they do. But, I felt awfully lonesome walking home alone. Most days I walk home with Bryan; yesterday, I didn't have time to feel lonesome. But today, I had all the time in the world.

Words don't help when you're walking home by yourself; instead, they just say the things that you don't want to think about and also elicit strange looks from people not talking to themselves, and some that are.

"Well, perhaps Bryan would be fine with the female... version of you."

I clucked my tongue at myself. "What would make you think that? He would probably freak out."

"He didn't freak out when I told him I was an alien."

"Well, that's different."

"How is it different?"

"I don't know."

I decided to reconveine my conversation once I got somewhere more private. It felt like Kevin and

Katerina were fighting, and I wasn't sure who was who.

"Hey."

I noticed right off that I wasn't the person to say that. I slowly turned around to look in the general direction of the sound. It was Bryan. Every peice of me told me to run, get away, but an equal part told me to explain everything. Again, I wasn't sure which was Kat and which was Kev.

Once he had caught up his face shifted into one of confusion. "Sorry, Kat. For a moment I thought you were Kevin." He shook his head a little. "I don't know why."

"It's okay." I tucked some hair behind my ear. I shifted in my skirt. It had felt awkward when I first put it on but that didn't even compare to the awkward feeling of the lack of cloth between my legs now. This was when I desperately wished I had slipped shorts on under my skirt.

He fell into step next to me. "So, you doing okay? You look like you're having trouble."

Honestly, I was still trying to process how we had started moving, let alone the fact that Bryan was speaking to me. Somehow, I heard what he had said. "Yeah, you wouldn't understand." Then I added, playfully. "You know, *girl* problems."

Bryan chuckled. "Which translated to you having *boy* troubles, yeah?"

I was surprised at how adept he was; he was much better at this than I had imagined. Maybe I should just talk to him in the female form forever, pretend Kevin never existed. "Yeppers."

His head clicked sideways a tad. I realized belatedly that I had just used a coined-Kevin-catch-phrase. "Well, you can always talk to me, I... actually, I don't feel like we just met yesterday. Funny isn't it?"

I chuckled dryly. "Yeah, funny."

His head popped back to look at me. "I'm sorry. Am I making you uncomfortable? If I am just say so." He brought his hands up into a surrender-like stance.

"No." I shook my head. "Not at all."

He breathed a sigh of what I could only fathom as relief. "Good. So, uh-"

He didn't get to finish whatever he was about to say. "Yelloh, red hed!"

I winced. I was trying to figure why so many people had stayed after school; it was like the school decided it was 'let's make Kevin-Katerina feel awkward and bring the First of April to the end of September.' I was starting to hope that this exempted me from the next April Fool's Day, but I don't think the universe works like that.

Stormy scooted inbetween Bryan and me. "Hello, to you too." She nodded curtly to me before looking back to Bryan. I then remembered that Stormy had never met Katerina, only Kev.

"Hello." I said back to her, a sudden surge of courage pulsing from wherever women get the extra snippyness from. "I'm Katerina, and I think you interrupted my conversation."

"I'm sorry." She said before turning away from me with a disgusted growl. "But, I believe that I've known Bryan longer, eh, New Girl?"

I ground my teeth together and contemplated what to say next. I had absolutely no clue what I could say that wouldn't make me a, well, you-know-what nor a push-over. But I didn't get the chance.

I had two unauthorized things happened to me at the same time. First, Stormy and Bryan started fighting, and I didn't have a chance to find out, because of the second thing: I started to tingle.

This was bad, very, very bad.

The tingles moved from the tips of my fingers and began to move up the edges of my arms and rested a moment or two in my elbows.

"You know you like the poor soul, just admit to it." Stormy picked at the bright green finger nail polish on her thumbnail. As it pulled away, it revealed a bright pink color underneath.

"I don't understand what you're talking about." Bryan breathed. I recognized the breath as that of when he is trying to keep his coo. You know, red heads have a temper and all that.

"I can see it all over your face." She swooped an index finger around the egdes of Bryan's face only a few centimeters from his skin.

Bryan's face turned bright red and I felt the burst of anger comin g on. It didn't help that the tingles were starting to make my shoulders shiver and I needed to get out of this group soon.

Stormy then leaned toward Bryan's ear sticking her rear end in my direction to counter balance. I looked down at her butt and decided that it was a horrible thing, the thong. It had rubbed all over my seat, the too-low of rise pants, all of it, her, I hated her. She whispered something that even I couldn't hear.

But Bryan had. He burst into a yelling tirade. "Would you just go back to wherever you came from and leave me alone?!?"

The tingles had become unbearable, not painful, just so sense-encompassing that I knew it wouldn't be long. So sense-encompassing in fact, that Stormy had to point out that there were tears running down my face.

"I'm sorry." I stuttered, I felt my throat doing some funny things, like any throat does when one cries. "I have to go."

I ran. I ran away from the two of them.

"Let go of me. You did all of this." I heard Bryan yell.

Then I heard Stormy's reply. "No, Bryan, you did this. You frightened the poor thing."

It was the last thing she said that reminded me of something very important.

"You frightened her so much she's gone running home."

I was having the worst luck. I couldn't run to my house, Bryan would see. Especially since they were rounding the corner to my street just as I had a moment before. This took some quick thinking.

Very quick thinking. And I am not good at quick thinking.

So I gave up on it all together and decided that I didn't care. I'd figure out an excuse in the morning.

I ran directly up to my house. Tried the door and found it unlocked, just like everyother day. I slammed the door behind me and lept up the stairs, two at a time. Mom stayed down in the innards of the house, wherever she was; and I sat up on my bed, not Katerina's bed, my bed, Kevin's bed, because by the time my face hit the covers, it was back to its old self. Male and underconfident and feeling awfully alone.

Mom came up to get me for dinner. I was still the worst son in the world. I was like the walking dead according to her.

"Honey, eat something substantial please. Two bites isn't enough to live on." She lifted another spoonful of goulash to her lips and ate it slowly, probably making one of the feminine thinking faces that I only understand when I'm female, as well.

She tutted at me and this time I knew she was making one of those faces.

"You want to talk about anything?"

I shook my head. But I guess my mouth didn't get the memo. I started to tell her everything. About Stormy breaking into the conversation, about me running here, about me not understanding her faces once again. I even mentioned the part where my mouth didn't get the memo from my brain.

She listened, like every good mom does. And she is one of the best mom's ever. "Sweetheart, what do you plan to tell him tomorrow, if he asks?"

I heaped an overfull spoonful of goulash into my mouth. "Yaye un-now." Again, I knew she was giving me one of those cryptic female looks. I swallowed. "I don't know. That's what I've been trying to figure out, but nothing sounds right."

She stirred her food around the blue plate. "Perhaps the truth?" She didn't even look at me, her eyes were trained onto the plate of food.

I sighed. "That's the only good explanation."

She shook her head. "I don't think there is a good explanation."

I scoffed lightly to myself.

She got up and filled her plate again; I still hadn't gotten through my first. "Do you think I could stay home from school tomorrow?"

"Not a chance." She looked at me and smiled wickedly.

Did I say she was the best mother? I would like to take back that comment, right now. Oh, on backsies not trade backs? Well, that's stupid.

I put my plate in the sink. She called after me. "There's more in the pot if you get hungry later, and I know you will. You hardly ate anything."

In my room, I pulled out my learning notebook. I was profoundly happy that it had been transferred to my girly backpack. I stared at the backpack for a moment before zipping it up and chucking it across the hall to the other room, *her* room.

I wasn't sure what about Katerina that Kevin didn't like. It's awkward to explain how it all felt in my head. That's what the note book was for; I was going to try to write it down. Perhaps then it would make sense.

I started with something profound and moved on from there.

I found myself in a place where I and I

were fighting.

I feel as though a piece of me doesn't

click with the other.

A larger form inside of me saw both

opinions objectively,

While each of the arguments debate on

which was better.

I hope that will make sense sooner or later.

I shut the notebook and slipped it into the bag, probably the one I would take the next day. My stomach growled and begrudgingly I walked downstairs to fill another plate full of goulash. I slumped onto the couch and decided to eat it there.

It wasn't long before the whole idea of telling Bryan seeped back into my conscious brain. My stomach felt sick and started to dance a mean jitterbug with its contents. I made my way back up to my bedroom and crawled into bed. I didn't bother to pull of my clothes, just crawled in and pretended that tomorrow would never come.

And if tomorrow never came, I wouldn't feel so lost.

Because no one feels lost in their dreams.

At least not as lost as when they're awake.

I was sitting on my bed, in my room, Kevin's room. I was waiting for someone and I didn't know who. I just sat there, staring at the door waiting for someone to find me.

The door swung open and Stormy walked in. She slid up beside me and pet my head; I felt like a dog.

"Oh, sweetheart." She said. "You wanted Bryan to come didn't you?"

I looked at her and I nodded. I had a funny feeling that he was exactly who I was waiting for.

"Well, what if I told you that you have me instead?"

I blinked. I then had another funny feeling, and I couldn't talk. I was completely stuck with whatever she decided. I really didn't like that.

"But, you like me, right? You liked my thong. You liked my hips." With each statement her face came closer and closer to mine. "You liked my stomach." Closer still. "You liked my legs." I felt like she was going to suffocate me.

No, I didn't, I thought. I liked you before I knew you.

She got even closer. "But you don't know me..." She stopped moving closer. She turned her head toward the door. "Oh, look who has come to join us."

I glanced toward the door, Bryan was there. He was red faced and breathing heavily. It was one of the sexiest things I had ever seen. "Get away from her."

"What do you mean?" Stormy chided. "This is Kevin."

"Get away from her." Bryan said again.

I felt my stomach tingle briefly and awaited the realization. The room morphed. It turned into the one across the hall, Katerina's room, but Stormy and Bryan were still there.

Stormy jumped up and wiped her hands on my bed. "Eww, you're a girl. Are you a freakin' transvestite or something?"

I wanted to say 'no' but I still couldn't say anything.

Bryan growled. "Stormy, get out."

"Sheesh, fine. You two have your transvestite, homosexual love. What do I even care?"

She stomped out of the room. Bryan heaved air in and out until his face wasn't as red.

"You shouldn't have." I whispered. It seemed that I could start talking, but it was barely louder than a breath.

"Why not?" Bryan moved closer, until he was sitting on the bed. The opposite side than Stormy had been on.

"You and I, we've been friends for so long. What would this do? It would ruin a friendship. It would ruin us. Then I would lose you. I don't want to lose you." Tears started to fall from my eyes. I wanted to curl up and pretend I was never there.

"Friends or no, I am not going to let you end up with Stormy."

"What?" I looked up at him.

His arms were open and he let me lean into him and curl into his chest. "You have a choice. Stormy or me, and I'm not going to let you pick Stormy." He ran a hand through my hair. It had nothing in common with how Stormy had patted my head. Bryan was gentler, kinder.

I grabbed his shirt and pulled it toward my nose so I could smell it. It was Bryan.

He lifted my face. "What do you say?"

"I say I don't want to be with Stormy."

"Then you'll be with me?"

I nodded. I grabbed his hand and we sat there. We sat there hand and hand.

"So, Katerina, where is Kevin?"

I froze.

"I am Kevin."

"Oh." That was all he said, absolutely all. And I felt extremely relieved. My room started to morph again and so did I. I was sitting there, as Kevin, holding Bryan's hand. He smiled at me. "I love you."

That's when I woke up.

I felt out of place, and as my mind woke up, I figured out exactly why. I threw the covers off of me, pulled off my pants and socks and headed to my room, across the hall.

My boobs pushed weirdly against the men's shirt and my butt filled in my boxers more but I didn't care, I just wanted to go to sleep and figure it all out in the morning.

CHAPTER NINE

The morning came too soon. I used my semi-normal routine, getting up, getting dressed, grabbing waffles on my way out. Complete with my female backpack, female legs, and female face.

On my way to school, I encountered some familiar faces. Namely, Bryan and Stormy, already bugging each other. I shivered. If last night's dream was true, then those were my choices.

Stormy: The girl who was horrible to everyone. Another word came to mind, but I don't swear.

Or.

Bryan: The sweet, endearing guy that I am starting to think I've always liked, but knows me as Kevin and that could be insanely weird.

I looked up to the sky. Why did You had to give me those two choices?

Bryan noticed me and waved. I gave him a small wave in return. By the smile on his face, he probably hadn't seen the house I ran into yesterday.

I moved a little faster; I wanted to look like I was trying to catch up without actually doing so.

When I was within earshot, I eavesdropped, purely on accident, but I didn't care. I am totally honest, I didn't.

"Well, this boyfriend of yours seems shifty. He hasn't shown up for two days. Maybe he's trying to say that he's dumping you."

I winced.

"No, Kevin's just going through some stuff; he'll turn up soon." Bryan looked really confident.

I wondered why. I also wondered why he was so open with her saying that I, er *Kevin*, was his boyfriend.

"Look, goldilocks is back. Well, actually indigolocks. Which is pretty cool but also really weird."

I humpfed and crossed my arms. She waved for me to catch up. I was starting to feel like this was going a lot better than it should have been. I moved toward them. "Good morning."

"Good morning." Bryan smiled sheepishly.

"Top o' the day." Stormy tipped an imaginary hat.

Now I was really perplexed.

"So why are you guys so nice all of a sudden?"

Stormy sighed like it was the most obvious thing in the world. "Because, the world is a much happier place today."

I grumbled. "Doesn't feel like it to me."

Bryan laughed awkwardly.

"You see," continued Stormy, "Rita asked me out last night."

I almost choked on air. "What?!?"

"You have a problem with homosexuals?" She turned on me with some sort of raw meat sparkling in her eyes. I had a feeling it was reflecting me after a skinning or something.

"Nope." Bryan quickly said. "Not at all."

"I wasn't talking to you, I was talking to her." She pointed at me.

"I have no problem with them."

Stormy's complexion was no longer stormy, but bright and sunny and meaningful. She skipped up the steps of the school and away from Bryan and I. I nodded, still perplexed, in her direction.

Bryan turned to me. "So, you want an escort to class?" He held out his arm to me.

I have no clue what came over me, but all I know is that it did. "Won't your boyfriend mind?"

He looked at me, then back toward the street we had walked down, my street. I swallowed.

"No, I think he'd be fine with it."

I was still absolutely baffled, but I took his arm and let him escort me to biology.

The bell rang, though, so the two of us had to run to class. Holding someone's arm doesn't work that way, so I grabbed his hand and took off. He laughed; so did I.

We got there and leaned onto a wall to support his heavier breathing and laughing. I leaned against the hall in front of him. He brought a hand up to my face. My eyes went wide; I knew it because my eyes suddenly got extremely dry, but that also maybe because the air around Bryan and I got a hundred times hotter in only about four seconds.

He noticed and stared at his hand then jumped, like he hadn't known what he was doing. The hand dropped to his side before being shoved deep into his pocket. "Sorry," he grumbled.

I shook my head. I didn't have any time to reassure him; Mr. Stewart peaked his head into the hall. "You two want to be late?"

I shook my head. I don't know what Bryan did; I wasn't paying attention.

"Then get in here." Mr. Stewart waved us into the classroom.

I was just glad that people were too busy talking to eachother instead of doing actual work. And I saw Stormy, sitting in *my* seat, just like she told me.

Before I could scan the room for another seat, though, Bryan pulled me to him and whispered into my ear. Using that husky, amazing voice, he said, "Meet me at the outdoor bleachers after school."

I nodded, but I'm not sure if he saw it. He was already heading over to sit in his spot, next to *my* spot, which currently belonged to Stormy.

I noticed movement toward the side of the room, though. Simon was waving and gesturing to an empty seat. Relieved, I sat next to him. He smiled and patted my back.

I grinned back.

Then I pulled out my notebook and resumed a dilly-dally thing called school.

Under normal circumstances, I would have made it through school with the disposition of a zombie on catnip but today seemed to be a lot different. It seemed that it was supposed to be a good day. Nothing could make me feel bad.

Stormy's taunting, Mrs. English Fascism's quiz, and, currently, Harley's chewing; none could quiet my mood.

I waited patiently for the clock, and that was a surprise. I listened intently to the conversaiton, or at least what I could hear of it over the chewing.

"So, it was just the other day, you know, at my 'house' and I was just waiting around." Simon took a swig from his water bottle. His voice got quieter. "And a giant fish came swimming towards me..." his voice altoed all over again, "it was the funniest thing you could have seen!"

Gina giggled and took a bite of her roast beef sandwich. A trail of red blood - it was very, very, rare roast beef - rolled down her arm. I watched, almost amused, when Simon reached over with a napkin to run it over her chin and arm. She smiled, her teeth glossed with red-liquid sheen.

Harley's chewing ceased, and for a moment, I wasn't sure if there was another noise –like how when a tone dissappears, you realized that you were so focused on the tone that you can't hear anything else for that moment– before I could listen to any of the cafeteria noises, though, Harley began chewing again.

I stifled a small laugh. I found it absolutely incredulous that all of this was happening. Only two days ago all of this would have been impossible, untrue, a joke; but now, this is real and miraculous.

I slipped a quick look toward Stormy, she sat next to Rita who was bundled up in her hoodie. Rita's polka-dots were a little bit larger than the day before and the way she was sitting made me feel bad. Stormy must have picked the sunniest table in the entire cafeteria, and Rita is sensitive to sunlight.

I wondered if any of the aliens had told anyone about their being alien. I would feel really bad if it turns out that most of them hadn't and that I broke an unsaid rule or something. I really didn't want that to be the case.

Someone tapped me on the shoulder. I jumped high enough to look Harley in the eyes; that must have been two feet or so. I turned to see Bryan standing there with a possum look.

I cleared my throat. "Yes?" I rubbed a hand against my forehead, haphazardly trying to move any wayward hairs.

"I was just wondering if I could sit with you?"

I felt the eyes of everyone sitting at the table on my back, probably boring small sockets into my back with a strange satisfaction. "I, uh..." I turn to Harley. Harley's mouth was clamped closed. I figure he didn't want Bryan to see the green, digestion-aiding mucus. I then turned to my other side where Simon continued to dibble at his food; Simon shrugged. "Sure, you can sit with us."

Everyone scooched inways and outways until there was room on the half-bench for Bryan to sit. Simon didn't stop picking at his food and Harley began to chew softer.

Bryan smiled. "So, how have you enjoyed the town?" He bit into a sloppy joe from the lunch line. I have always wondered if perhaps there was somthing alien about the lunch ladies or at least the food they tended to serve. I was told yesterday that the answer is no; but I still can't help but wonder if perhaps it's in their lineage somewhere forgotten by time.

I took a bite from the bagel sandwich I had brought to school. "Izzzz okaugh." I swallowed then tried again. "It's okay."

Bryan took another bite of sloppy joe. I wasn't sure if the entire table was paying attention to us or not but I was pretty confident that the other sittees were not conversing anymore. If only they understood how good of a guy Bryan was and that he would probably understand the whole alien thing, he understood me. Except for the whole not talking to him as if I were Kevin in forever.

Bryan looked around the cafeteria before turning back to me. "So, would you like to come over and work on schoolwork? Or just hangout?"

I was seriously trying not to think of the dream I had a few days before. You know, him and Kat sitting on the couch and everything? Or the other one, where he accepted me for me. But, now was not the place to think of confessing. I was in front of a gaggle of aliens -I looked it up the other night, I was deciding between using cete, sleuth, or gaggle as the term for a group of aliens- and even worse, in front of the majority of the school.

I was getting antsy and so was Bryan, I could tell. He had the little twitch in his fingers and a small bop to his leg. I didn't really want to wait until the bleachers nor did I want to extend my immediate family-in-secret.

I swept hair out of my face again. "So, uh, would you like to, uh..." I could feel the heat of some unknown inner sun rise up in my face, chest, and arms. I was hoping though that no one could tell. I heard a few snickers that told me otherwise. "Wannagooutsideforawhile?"

Bryan's face stretched out and I tried again.

"Want to go outside for a while?"

Bryan grinned. "Sure."

I dropped my bag on the front steps of the school, the same steps that Bryan and I ran up this morning. I found it daunting that I was to have the conversation *here* with Bryan. I could see my street. I could almost see Bryan's house. You couldn't see another shopping area because that was on the other side of the school.

Bryan sat down next to me and set his bag on the step below. I turned to him.

He didn't look at me. He stared out. "You seem awfully familiar, you know that?"

I swallowed.

"Like we've been friends forever but neither of us knew it."

I breathed. I definitely knew it; he was the one that didn't know it.

"I feel like I've been waiting for you." Bryan blushed.

I swallowed. "What if you have been?"

Bryan looked at me with a confused expression. I felt like I was being a horrible person for not out rightly tell him nor being consistent with not telling him.

I felt like it was the time to tell him. It was semi-secluded and sort of special.

"Miss Fryer."

I didn't turn. I just looked at Bryan, but Bryan turned to look.

"Miss Fryer."

That was when I realized that the voice was addressing me. I swiveled slowly, trying to perserve as much of the previous moment as I could. "Yes."

"Will you come see me in my office?" Only then did I recognize the voice. It was Doctor Petrov, or in that instant, my brain decided to call her Doctor Cockroach.

I sighed and got up off the step. I ruffled Bryan's hair before trailing, unwillingly, after Principle Petrov.

Doctor Petrov closed the door to her office with a thud and a click. She then motioned for me to sit down. She walked slowly to her chair. I noticed then that she was moving a little off, as if inside her skin there were actually two leg stuctures in each leg. It probably wasn't noticeable to someone who had never had the traumatizing experience of seeing her turn into a clear-exoskeletened bug.

"Katerina, I was hoping you could tell me some more about yourself."

I let my face scruch into some horrid form, probably nothing like the form Petrov coud take, but hopefully somewhere close. "What do you mean?"

"I would like to conclude what kind of alien you are so that I can have any necessities brought as soon as possible." Doctor Petrov looked at me over the nails she was picking at. It was a highly frightening experience.

"Um, okay," I swallowed. Doctor Petrov scared me, a lot. "I can now change at will, I think."

"Oh, good." She smiled warmly. She pressed a small red button on her intercom stand. "Please call Coach Crawford; I need to see him ASAP." There was no reply. Only the crackle of recieving then silence. "Anything else?" She directed her attention to me again.

I shook my head; I felt like I had made a terrible mistake and I was going to be punished for it.

She nodded slowly and moved behind the desk. "You may go now." Her voice was directed at the door more than toward me.

I backed away. I felt for the door knob and gave it a quick turn. Something about how the entire meeting happened, sounded, looked, *something*, had me nervous and half-way expecting that the door was locked and I would be mutilated or eaten very shortly.

The door knob creaked but turned completely and I opened the door. I slowly moved out of the room. It was not the best ending to a meeting, but it was definitely better than being eaten.

Coral followed me home from school; and though I didn't mean to be following Stormy and Rita and a little bit of Bryan, we were all going in the same direction at incremented times. I was busy watching Rita, with her large white hoodie, trying to stay wrapped up without drawing atttention to herself. It was awkward for Stormy though; she seemed to want to hold Rita's hand and Rita wouldn't comply.

I spent most of the walk home giggling slightly at the way Rita was conducting her relationship.

"You know, I don't really advocate interspecial relationships." Coral said.

I turned to look at her; a wall of purple hair got in the way so I threw it up into a bun-ponytail thing. "Why not?"

Coral flicked her head in my direction. "Oh, sorry, I didn't mean to think aloud." She shifted her bookbag, looking awkwardly at the sidewalk.

"But since you did, why don't you elaborate?"

Coral nodded. "It's just, what if in the future, the gene pools are so mixed that interstellar wars are brought to Earth or something? What if thenext gerneration' species can no longer fight infection or it compromises the offspring's chance of survival in another way?"

I never thought about any of that. I mean, I had thought of the fact that other planets and life exist, but it had always escaped me that it wasn't all peaceful. That cohabitation, like on Earth, wasn't everywhere. "What if that's why you're here?"

Coral looked at me and tilted her head. "To compromise life?"

I stopped and set a hand on either hip. "No. I mean, to repopulate, to survive, to escape war."

Coral thought about it. She kept walking and I followed. She was very quiet. That was when I realized that Coral didn't actually breathe. She wasn't taking in air or exhaling; she was just walking, and, hopefully, thinking.

While we continued down the sidewalk, I watched Rita and Stormy cross the street and enter her house. I could almost feel them walk up the stairs to Stormy's room just before a light from her window turned on.

"You know," Coral finally said, "I think that one of those reasons is why most of us are here."

I turned back to her. We started up the walkway to my house when I felt another sensation, like I had only moments earlier. A movement that I couldn't see. Someone was moving in my house and it wasn't my mom. And they were coming toward the door.

"Come on!" I grabbed Coral and ducked into a bush next to the small porch. The person moved to the door and I could feel, somewhere in my gut, the knob move.

"What are we doing?" Coral tried to move out of the bush.

"Shhh, wait!" I yanked her back in.

All I could see were the shoes of the person that left my house, but I would've recognized them anywhere. Orange converse shoes; identical to those worn by the one person in the world that couldn't be confusing me more than he already was: Bryan.

"Are you sure that I can't see him?" Bryan sounded pitiful.

Through the small gap between the door frame and the door I could see the feet of our green and yellow hasmat suit. "Sorry sweetie. I'm not quite sure what he has yet, but I know the symptoms. If you feel yourself bloating in the eyes or have severe cravings for chocolate, carrots, fish or eel tell your mother to call me, okay?"

I didn't hear a reply, so I assumed he nodded.

"Well, uh, could you tell Kevin that I was here?"

Again, there was no reply, so I assumed that my mom nodded.

Bryan turned and walked away. Once he was halfway down the front walkway, I could see him, shoulders hunched over, feet dragging, looking worn out.

"Come on out now; I thought he'd never leave."

Coral burst from the bush and put a hand on her chest. She closed her eyes then opened them and calmed herself. "Sorry, that was terrifying."

I looked at her and raised an eyebrow. I moved into the house automatically, watching Coral catch her 'breath'. "What's wrong?"

Coral shook her head dismissively. "I have trouble cycling whenever there is a single color." She blinked again. "Oh, or if there is too much white."

I nodded and made a mental note to ask about light and color and cycling later, after Coral caught her photons.

I walked into the kitchen and filled a glass with water and took it to Coral. She accepted it gratefully and gulped down all of it in one go. It took some major self control to not chant 'chug'.

We filed into the kitchen and I motioned for Coral to place her glass in the sink. I caught notice of something on the counter, next to the fridge though.

"Uh, Kat..."

I ignored her for the moment and walked over to the 'something'; it was a note.

"Kat..."

It was a note of five words, some of the scariest words in the world at that moment.

Be back soon. Love, Mom.

CHAPTER TEN

I woke up in the school building.

I didn't really remember what had happened.

I couldn't move; I wasn't tied up or anything, but my body was stuck to the floor —or I was just too heavy to move. A door opened somwhere, not a normal door, one of the doors that you see in a science fiction movie, a vacuum-sealed, sliding door.

The hazmat suit moved through it. I noticed that the suit didn't walk, didn't step, it sort of floated along the ground. I stared at the suit, the green and yellow hazmat suit that my mother had worn to care for alien-sick three-year-old me. It took forever to become comfortable with the tinted-out face. After that experience, I had a feeling that it would take just as long if not longer to get used to it again, as so far, I was terrified.

"You," the hazmat suit said, "how did you escape The Empire's Army?"

"The what?" I tried to shift to see the suit better. I realized that part of my discomfort was that I was in my boy form again, but in girl clothes. Female underwear, wonderful- note the sarcasm.

"The Empirial Fleet was sent to exterminate all of you pests, take down your family tree, drive an axe through its trunk." The Suit moved around me.

I had the slightest feeling that gravity wasn't working correctly. "Your race is all but felled out of existence, yet here you are."

"And here you are." I wiggled around a bit but the floor seemed to love me; and, in the process, I wedged my underwear into my buttcrack. Female underwear, worst invention ever. How girls wear thongs escapes me.

"Yes, here I am. An outcast, a criminal; on this prison world, a penal place for my race. Yet you walk amoung them with skill and grace; filth in filth."

I was not happy, to say the least. "My race is being exterminated by toxins, not by war." I laid still this time, as my predicament wasn't going to magically get better. I reached into my pocket and dug out my phone.

The being in the hazmat suit turned and walked toward the door. Hands were clasped at the small of its back.

I felt around the key pad. It was at this moment I thanked my mother for buying me a phone, even though I never use it. Small towns are usually small enough that a phone call is actually slower than gossip and word of mouth.

I found redial, and I pressed down on it, hard.

The hazmat suit float-turned again. "Your race isn't good enough for a war with battles and weapons."

"You mean that they're not worth a chance." I struggled again. I managed to turn onto my back with my hand and phone slightly behind me. I felt the keypad for some sort of speaker-phone button; photographic memory aiding me tremendously. "They weren't even allowed to have hope?"

The Hazmat Suit moved in my direction. "Hope is a demeaning thing. It is ingenic, it goes against all that my race allows. It is false when it is about war against my race. No race wins once we decide to move in."

I find the speaker-phone button; I push it. "Do you move in with toxins, like exterminators, or armor, like soldiers?"

The Hazmat Suit sneered at me. "We are warriors!"

"That exterminate vermin?"

"You little girl, boy, 〆 ♊ 𝔸𝔸, -⋮ ♋ ♂ ⋗ ♋ 〆 ♊ 𝔸𝔸 -need to shut your mouth." The hazmat suit - I can honestly say that in my head I started to call it Hazzy - moved its tinted face into mine. "You are just as lost as I feel." He sounded surprised and dumbfounded, almost sorry.

He was giving up the upper hand, so I smiled. "Yet. you are superior?" I moved the phone a little to make sure it received the next bit. "Hiding out in a school, are you waiting patiently or cowardly?"

"Warriors do not need patience, they need strength!" Hazzy pumped an arm into the air. I felt that the statement was true enough; I was hardly a warrior and there I sat, waiting.

I watched Hazzy move to the door again, walk through, and close it behind its yellow butt. I hadn't yet decided whether Hazzy was male or female or whether it was politically correct to assign a sex to a hazmat suit.

A long tone vibrated through the room, a small red light turned on, and the gravity turned off. Suddenly, I was floating around trying to reach my phone, which was also floating, but in the opposite direction as myself.

A second tone reverberated. I reached frantically for my phone; I was afraid that the tone meant that Hazzy was coming back. I still couldn't reach the phone.

A blue light flooded the chamber and a tingle began to ripple from my stomach. I started to become female. I had never completely experienced the change; I had either been crying or sleeping during the other times, otherwise emotionally preoccupied.

Being aware was creepy.

It was like my brain was twisting in knots; not that it hurt, just a sort of rerouting. It was like my chest had suddenly become water balloons and my hair like a wind up doll. The color was the best thing to watch, though; once the hair was long, the ripple moved through it, changing the color in a series of waves starting at the tips and ending with a small pinch in my scalp.

The worst part was the inside stuff. It felt like my insides had become noodles and jelly and were being whisked around. I felt like I was going to be sick and it didn't help that I was floating around.

I thought I was going to throw up, everywhere, anywhere. I waited through it, like some sort of withdrawal victim. I understood very little about what was happening in me but it felt weird and funny and disporportionate.

I was still reaching for my phone with one hand, holding my topsy-turning stomach with the other.

The lights in the room flickered before switching out and creating an eerie green color. My hair was caught in my clothes and my shirt had ridden up, so I was starting to feel a chill along my sides. I had never noticed it before but it looked like I had small purple freckles along my sides and stomach.

I twisted violently. Somewhat to help me work off some adrenaline, somewhat for no reason at all, and even more somewhat to try to get my phone that was still sending the call.

"You have to get help." I whispered. I hoped it was loud enough for the other person in our one-sided conversation to hear.

Then the phone made a small click sound.

I stared at it.

I hoped that it was not the person hanging up.

Then, though, the dialtone sounded.

Whoever it was, I was going to kill them, if I ever saw them again, if I ever figured out who it was.

I don't even know whose number was the last dialed, let alone if that was the person who answered.

A tone sounded again, and green light filled the chamber, and if earlier experience prooved true, that mean that gravity was about to make a comeback with more intensity than ever. I fell toward the floor, landing on the surface and sticking to it, my hair splayed out in every direction and stuck under me in awkward places making it pull at my scalp. I'd traded a wedgey for a headache.

This was when I realized that the dialtone was still sounding; and the phone was out of reach. I looked over to it, laying on its side, its white screen staring at me. It was sad, just like me, moaning about its problems.

The door opened with a suctioning sound. I didn't look over to it; I couldn't the way my head was plastered to the floor. I watched as two yellow

112

feet, hanging, dangling from the body of Hazzy, entered my peripheral vision. The feet moved to just above my phone. A yellow, shiny, rubbery hand reached toward the phone and picked it up carefully. "Your bombing device did not work. It will not work in this chamber; there is a peace force shiild, so you are unable to detonate weapons in this room." Hazzy's blacked out face turned toward me. "Even you should have known that."

I wasn't sure how to respond, but I gave it my best shot. "It's currently hacking your system. It will break down the shield soon."

"It'shighly fortified; this puny device will not work. Read the signs." Hazzy pointed to the ceiling of the chamber.

I forced my head into a position from whichI could read the ceiling. All I saw there were weird squiggles; some curly and some angle-y and some dotsies. It looked like gibberish to me. I didn't want Hazzy to know that though. "Oh, you have that system. That will be easy to hack."

Hazzy shook his head. "Unhackable."

I was losing confidence in the many sci-fi thrillers I had memorised. Nothing was working. Suddenly, Hazzy began to convulse. I looked over at it. "Are-are you okay?" Not exactly the best question to ask a being that wants you dead.

"What is this?!" Hazzy yelled at the top of his lungs, or gills, or sacks, or whatever he was speaking with. "It was unhackable." Hazzy groaned out through his spasms.

Then I began to hear faint music coming from under Hazzy. It was some obscure song from an even more obscure sci-fi film, that I happened to love.

That's when I realized, my phone had gone off; someone was calling me. Gravity started to turn off and I was able to stand up, though I still felt heavy. I moved to the deflated hazmat suit and flipped it over, away from my phone. The small screen read 'Home'. I aswered it. "Hello."

The phone didn't give off any sound. Instead, the P.A. system- or something like it that used tubes filled with greenish liquid to give off sounds, which I thought was really cool- ground out a somewhat muffled version of my mother's voice, like she were underwater. "Hey," gurgle, "where are you? I came home and," gurgle, gurgle "here."

"I'm fine, Mom."

I waited for her to answer. Gurgle, "are you there?"

"Yeah, Mom, I said I was fine."

I waited again. "Can you hear me?" There was a pause, "Because I can't hear you."

I sighed and hung up. No use trying to get her to hear me if I couldn't find or use a speaker.

I looked down at Hazzy. The suit was deflated and just laying there, the being inside either dead, passed out, or some other state that I wasn't aware existed. I also decided that my mom could buy a new hazmat suit.

I walked toward the door and peeked out. There was a long hallway with about 12 different doors. I wasn't sure if the doors were supposed to look the way they did but they looked really weird. Each looked like a geode or like how motor oil looks when floating on water. I walked up to one and placed a hand on it. My phone beeped.

I looked at my phone, conveniently in my other hand. I opened it. Across the screen was more of the weird language that was on the ceiling of the gravity-changing chamber. The text stopped after a moment, clearing the screen.

I wasn't sure what my phone was doing but I was a little scared that it had become some sort of smart phone, at least smart enough to understand a language that I hadn't a clue about.

Then the gurgling speech came back. "Press One to continue through Door One. Press Star for more Options."

I looked around. Smiled really wide to myself. Then I pressed one.

The door opened. Behind it was a forest. I watched wide-eyed before pressing one again.

I smiled and looked around again. Then I pressed Star. The P.A. System gurgled again. "For the Banquet Room, press Three." I looked at the next door; food sounded really good. "For the Control Room, press Four." I looked at the door beyond three. "To hear more options press Star." I looked down at the screen and there was a small map of, what I'm guessing is, a ship. I walked forward, the map shifted forward. I moved so that doors 5, 6, and 7 were on the display. I pressed Star.

"To enter the Library, press 5; to enter the Bounce Hall, press 6; to leave ship, press 7." I didn't even think about it; I pressed seven.

I was suddenly a little scared of what I had done. A twisting sensation overtook my stomach, worse than the sex-changing-sickness. I felt my ears pop and my body squish together. My entire body hurled toward door 7.

Then, I was in a supply closet. The smell of bleach and mop water hit my nose and tears welled up from the pungent odor. I coughed, loud, and tried to turn the handle. The door wouldn't move; it was locked.

"Hello? Who's there?"

I jumped. Just on the otherside of the door was a person.

"Kevin, is that you?" It was Bryan.

I coughed a bit more, but managed to reply. "It's Katerina, could you get me out?"

"Sure."

He opened the door and I smiled as Bryan, the dorky redhead that lived down my street came into view. I jumped at him, hugging him. "Thank you, thank you. Why are you here?"

"Kevin called." Bryan coughed quietly; I probably smelled like bleach and other cleaning supplies.

I swallowed, hoping it wasn't noticeable. "Really?"

"Yeah. How did you get in the closet?"

I looked back at the closet door, trying to think of a good answer. I went with the truth. "I have no clue."

Bryan laughed. I smiled and laughed, too.

The laughter died slowly and I noticed that the school was dark and the windows were as well. "What time is it?"

"Almost 10, I think." Bryan pulled out his cell phone to check. I didn't even bother looking at mine; it seemed to no longer do basic functions. Bryan flashed the screen at me. "Yep, see."

I nodded and looked around. "So how did you get in?"

Bryan chuckled. "Through the Girl's Locker Room window."

We laughed again and walked toward the Girl's Locker Room.

Once outside and walking home, I realized that he never 'helped Kevin,' the person he went there to save. I swallowed. "What about Kevin?"

Bryan looked down at the ground. "I have a feeling he's safe." He scuffed a shoe through a step or two. "I mean, I should ask you, right Katerina?"

I stopped walking abruptly. "What do you mean?"

Bryan sighed. "Kat?" He pointed at me with his arm outstretched.

I stared blankly at him.

He recoiled his arm then jabbed it at me again. "Kevin."

I just looked at him. I swallowed again. "Hey." I sounded pitiful. "Would you look at that." I took a deep breath then let it out. "Wonder how that happened."

Bryan looked at me, not meeting my eyes, instead awkwardly stopping at my chin. "I'm not sure I want to know."

For some reason that broke the tense atmosphere in half. We both just laughed, and laughed, and laughed some more. Once we both caught our breath, I began to walk. Bryan holds up a hand and looks suspiciously behind me.

I don't dare turn around. I'm a little scared that I'd find out it was a flock of aliens all trying to kill me.

He flipped his hand over and cautiously motioned that I move forward. I creeped forward.

He blinked. "What is that? Is there a puddle following you?"

I blinked a few times, trying to make sense of what he said, but then realized that without seeing what he meant, it probably wouldn't make sense. So I turned around.

There was a puddle a few sidewalk squares behind me.

I took a step backward. The puddle stayed the same distance away, moving onto the next square. It moved like a shadow, but it wasn't attached to anything.

"If you're here to kill me, stay back. I'm armed and dangerous." I struck a Kung Fu pose.

Bryan stepped beside me and leaned down. "What?"

"Shhhhhhh."

Bryan just stared at me like I was crazy. I could feel his gaze on the side of my head. But I had to worry about the puddle.

I waited a few seconds, long seconds. Made sure that the puddle had ample time to decide what it wanted to do and either scurry away or attack or whatever it is moving puddles do. In retrospect, I realized that I am a really trusting person and a few seconds should not have been enough time for me to give my trust to a moving puddle, but I did.

My Kung Fu pose melted into a normal pose, a person standing dumfounded looking at a puddle. Bryan kept staring, though. "What? I was captured by an alien who wanted to kill me or something. I'm allowed to be suspicious." I stuck my hands on my hips.

"No, I understand that. I was just trying to figure out what kind of stupid it would take for something to believe that you're dangerous." He smirked.

I scrunched up my nose at him. I knew he was joking. He smiled and I smiled back.

I licked my lips. "So, what do you think it is?"

Bryan shrugged. "I dunno." He walked toward it. He stopped in the sidewalk square just before it. He squatted down to look at it. "It looks like a puddle of rainbows."

"Really?" I walked toward it, too. It didn't move this time. Bryan reached toward it. "Don't touch it." My phone stated to vibrate. I pulled it out and flipped it open.

Across the screen it read, 'Proximity Alert, No Lifeforms on Board,' underneath was a scrolling list: 'Press One to enter ship, Press two to engage weapons systems, Press Three to ignore, Press Four...'

"Oh." I clicked three then stuck my phone into my pocket. "It seems that it's my spaceship."

Bryan straightened up. "You have a space ship now? When did this happen?"

I smiled and shrugged. "Just recently."

CHAPTER ELEVEN

"Then my phone just sort of worked as a leash and brought it home with me." I explained for the last time to my mom and Bryan. It had taken the promise of pizza to get Bryan to stop asking about the ship long enough so that I could get home. I figured Mom would want to know and that I would get very frustrated repeating the same story multiple times.

Mom nodded. "So that's why I couldn't hear you."

I nodded back.

Bryan cleared his throat. "Then why could I hear you?"

I shrugged. "My best guess is that my calling you didn't breech the system, but the dial tone had."

"Well, I find it interesting that an alien's Spaceship runs on tones. You'd think that someone could sing and get out very easily." Mom ran a finger around her hot cocoa mug.

I smiled.

Mom smiled back. "I'm glad you're not hurt. I'm glad that I wasn't worrying for no reason, though." She sipped her Cocoa. "I almost called the police."

I smiled wider. "Thanks, Mom."

Bryan turned in his chair to look at the puddle/spaceship sitting in the middle of the rug. "So, will it follow you forever?"

I shook my head and pulled out my phone. I opened to the screen and waited for the end of the scrolling list. I gestured for Bryan to look. 'Press seven to make invisible; press eight to make this a permanent spot;press nine to enable autopilot; for more options, press Star.'

Bryan nodded. Then I showed Mom the same thing.

She nodded slowly and sipped her cocoa some more.

There was only one question left, on my part anyway. "Can I keep it?"

Coral handed my phone back. My phone ended up becoming one of the best alien thingy-ma-bobbers a stranded alien could ask for. It had four different alien-Language-to-English-Language Dictionaries and vice versa. It had a camera, so if I took a picture of something, it would translate it. It was the spaceship's remote and, after some fiddling, it could make calls again.

"That is pretty cool." Coral smiled.

Coral, myself, and the entire SC - Skeptic Club, the renamed AA -, were sitting in the forest room of my spaceship on small picnic mats. We had become pretty good friends and seemed to be having a fair enough time trying to make sense of alien life on Earth.

"I kinda don't have anything from my alien childhood." I ran my thumb along my phone.

Rita looked up. "It's okay. At least you weren't forced by your mother to bring something like this." She held up what I thought was one of the cutest pictures: it was a younger version of her, still with her black speckles, though.

"I think it's cute." Gina smiled; she cuddled with what she said was one of her most prized dolls from her home planet. It had been her only possession there.

Rita glared at Gina, then at the picture and shrugged.

Coral clapped. "Well, that's it for today, I guess. Kevin, could you take us home?"

I nodded and flipped open my phone. I pressed the seven key. My insides churned, just as they had the first time, but since then I'd grown more accustomed to it. I knew it was coming instead of being surprised like that first time.

All of us appeared in my bedroom, just outside of my closet, where the spaceship was planted in the wall behind my clothes.

Mom didn't mind having it there. She was just happy that it came with a full alien laboratory that she could access. It also came with more of the toxin and some futile alien attempts at making an antidote. She seemed ecstatic with the whole thing and she was closer than ever to a cure.

She was still usually in the basement but more often than not, she'd come up to have dinner with me and sometimes even sit at the table in the morning.

I showed everyone to the door, where Bryan seemed to have let himself in and taken over our couch. He had a bag of potato chips and a pair of sodas on the side table.

Once everyone was gone, I stood between him and the T.V. "You just going to eat our food now?"

He shrugged and tried to look around me. "It's not like you guys ever eat it."

"Yes, we do." I said defiantly. He was right, though; we either ate at someone else's house or ate take-out food most of the time, except for hot cocoa, that was sort of our special thing.

I sat down next to Bryan. He shifted so I could sit comfortably. We hadn't gotten together, but we hadn't not gotten together, either. Bryan and I had decided to just see what happens. And seeing what happens was probably the best plan.

Bryan handed me a soda and shifted closer to me.

Sometimes, I wondered if he was pushing boundaries just to tease me, because I couldn't completely control the genderswitch thing. Other times, I figured he was just seeing whether he liked it or not.

He scooted closer to me. Then closer again.

I could feel the change start, in my toes and my scalp; then the organ omelet formed and all-in-all, I became Kat again.

Bryan patted me on the head and smiled.

I smiled, too. Being an alien wasn't that bad.

Even in a small town, where everyone knew everything.

Well, I looked at Bryan, then settled into his side, almost everything.

I am
And I will be
And there
I have
Time

You are
And you will be
Hopefully
Near me
There

I know me
You know you
Together
Strong are
We

Printed in Great Britain
by Amazon

49236140R00079